SPY CLASSROOM

01

code name
MEADOW

code name
**DAUGHTER
DEAREST**

code name
KLAUS

code name
DREAMSPEAKER

code name
FORGETTER

code name
GLINT

code name
PANDEMONIUM

code name
**FLOWER
GARDEN**

A Girl on a Mission

SPY 01
CLASSROOM

Lily of the Garden

Takemachi
ILLUSTRATION BY: **Tomari**

YEN
ON
New York

SPY CLASSROOM ⁰¹

Translation by Nathaniel Thrasher
Cover art by Tomari
Assistance with firearm research: Asaura

SPY KYOSHITSU Vol.1 <<HANAZONO>> NO LILY
©Takemachi, Tomari 2020
First published in Japan in 2020 by KADOKAWA CORPORATION, Tokyo.
English translation rights arranged with KADOKAWA CORPORATION, Tokyo through TUTTLE-MORI AGENCY, INC., Tokyo.

Yen On
150 West 30th Street
New York, NY 10001

Visit us at yenpress.com
facebook.com/yenpress
twitter.com/yenpress
yenpress.tumblr.com
instagram.com/yenpress

First Yen On Edition: August 2021

Yen On is an imprint of Yen Press, LLC.
The Yen On name and logo are trademarks of Yen Press, LLC.

Library of Congress Cataloging-in-Publication Data
Names: Takemachi, author. I Tomari, Meron, illustrator. I Thrasher, Nathaniel Hiroshi, translator.
Title: Spy classroom / Takemachi ; illustrated by Tomari ; translation by Nathaniel Thrasher.
Other titles: Spy kyoushitsu. English
Description: First Yen On edition. I New York, NY : Yen On, 2021.
Identifiers: LCCN 2021021119 I ISBN 9781975322403 (v. 1 ; trade paperback)
Subjects: I CYAC: Spies—Fiction. I Schools—Fiction.
Classification: LCC PZ7.1.T343 Sp 2021 I DDC [Fic]—dc23
LC record available at https://lccn.loc.gov/2021021119

ISBNs: 978-1-9753-2240-3 (paperback)
          978-1-9753-2241-0 (ebook)

10 9 8 7 6 5 4 3 2 1

LSC-C

Printed in the United States of America

CONTENTS

SPY CLASSROOM

Specialized lessons for an impossible mission

Code name: Flower Garden

A spy always lies.

Prologue

Special Assignment

Guido stood in front of a room. He was the direct supervisor of the man inside, and both were members of the spy team Inferno working for the Din Republic.

Every member of Inferno was an oddball in some way or another, but that one marched to the beat of an especially unique drum. Guido, who possessed at least a semblance of common sense, had been tasked with getting in touch with him.

I guess you reap what you sow. Guido sighed.

He was the one who first took the man in. He had taken care of the young orphan and then raised him into an elite spy. However, he had never imagined that the boy would grow up to be such a handful.

His subordinate had been holed up in his room since morning. He hadn't come out for breakfast, for lunch, or to even use the bathroom.

What the hell is he up to in there? Guido wondered in exasperation. He began knocking. After five seconds passed with no answer, he stopped knocking and just opened the door.

The state of the quarters filled him with horror.

The bedroom had been decorated with elegant white wallpaper and a beautiful red carpet—but now everything was drowned in crimson.

A liquid resembling fresh blood had been splattered across the room and covered everything from the bed to the clothing shelves. It was like a murder scene. Even Guido, who was no stranger to death, almost screamed. A room in this beautiful manor, Heat Haze Palace, had been reduced to a ghastly spectacle.

And in the center of it all stood a giant canvas with a man lingering before it. He was gazing at the painting, spellbound. "Magnificent."

He swung his brush like a cudgel, sending paint flying across the canvas, the carpet, and eventually, Guido's face. That was when the artist noticed Guido's presence and turned around.

"Hmm? ...Master, what are you doing in here?"

"What are *you* doing in here?"

"I was struck by a sudden urge to draw. And I'm running out of paint, so could you get me some more?"

"...What, you're gonna use your mentor as your errand boy?" Guido shot back. "Cut the shitty jokes; I'm here about something serious."

Although, given who he was talking to, there was a good chance that it hadn't been a joke at all.

"You've got a special assignment. Starting tomorrow, you're going to split off from the rest of the team and carry out a solo mission."

"Special how...?"

Guido began laying out the mission. As his explanation progressed, his subordinate's expression began to change. The mission was harsh enough that just hearing its particulars would have been enough to send any ordinary spy into a blustering rage. Even Guido, skilled as he was, would have rejected it on the spot. These might as well have been orders to go out and die a meaningless death.

"Odds of success will be sub–ten percent, even for you. Failure will mean death. Can you do it?"

The man gave his answer without hesitating. "If that's the order, then I'll see it done."

Guido had fully expected a no; he stared in blank amazement.

The artist swept his brush across the canvas once more, smearing it red. "That should do it for today," he murmured, then nodded and looked Guido in the eye.

"Master, in case I don't make it, I want to leave you my last testament. Everything I am today is thanks to you. You took me in as an orphan and raised me to be a spy. I'll be forever grateful to the boss for hiring me, and it's no exaggeration to say I love each and every member of Inferno. I might not know my parents, but I think of you all as my family. And those family members all have friends, lovers, and relatives. And because those are the people who make up this nation, then I love this nation as well."

"You're not thinkin' of just making a break for it?"

"Not even a little."

Guido took a deep breath. Things would have been so much easier if the guy had simply refused. "What an idiot of a pupil I've raised. Look, when you finish your mission, I have a title for you to introduce yourself as."

"What kind of spy goes around introducing himself?"

It was an oddly reasonable question coming from him, but Guido chose to ignore it.

The Greatest Spy in the World.

The moniker was downright childish—but the spy in question seemed to take quite a liking to it.

"Magnificent."

Deciding to set out at once, the man cleaned up his painting utensils, changed into a new suit, and loaded it up with weapons. His wristwatch had wire inside for strangling people, his fountain pen had a built-in voice recorder, his collar had a razor blade hidden in it, and his sleeves were full of long needles.

After his subordinate finished prepping (in under five minutes), Guido gave him some parting words.

"Good luck out there."

The man's eyes widened, as if he were perplexed by the unusual pep talk.

After a brief pause, an embarrassed smile spread across his face.

"…See you when I get back."

Chapter 1

Coercion

The world was awash in pain.

The war was simply called the Great War, a conflict on a scale never before seen, and it had left the world with bitter pain and unhealed scars. The Galgad Empire's surrender had marked the end of the bloodshed, but even the victorious nations had lost tens of millions of their people. In a very real sense, it was a war with no true winners.

The Great War was also particular in that the majority of its casualties were civilians.

Gone was the era of bows and swords. This was the era of scientific progress, and the lethality of a single weapon put everything from olden times to shame. Submachine guns, poison gas, fighter jets, land mines... To put it frankly, it had become too easy to kill people. In the war's final stages, when both sides had completely lost perspective, countless indiscriminate massacres had been carried out. Most of those targeted had been women and children with no means of defending themselves.

After seeing what the war had wrought, the world's politicians came to a realization.

From a cost-benefit standpoint, war simply was not a feasible option.

And at the end of the day, it was only one of many possible measures they could take to resolve a conflict.

If they could achieve their ends through other means, then why not just do that?

There was no need to go to war over the right to drill for petroleum in a hostile nation. It was far more efficient to get that nation's politicians to just sign a treaty allowing it, and there was no shortage of ways that could be achieved. They could kidnap their families, they could bribe them with money and asylum, or they could have women seduce them and gain control of them that way. And if a politician was getting in their way, they could fabricate scandals to remove them from office or simply assassinate them. Either would be far more efficient than starting a war that would cost millions of lives.

Even if peace was just a pretense, that was good enough.

In the wake of the Great War, the nations of the world signed various peace treaties and established an international organization dedicated to maintaining order around the globe. At that organization's first summit, leaders from all across the world got together and shook hands while smiling radiantly.

That marked the end of wars fought in the light.

Now spies and information were the currency of conflict—of shadow wars.

The Din Republic was one of the countries that had suffered in the Great War.

It was a rural nation, one that would have been perfectly happy staying out of the fray entirely. After being left behind by the rapid advances of the industrial revolution, the Din Republic continued dutifully producing high-quality agricultural crops. It didn't have the military to expand itself through colonial rule, and it lacked the natural resources to invite foreign aggression. But the Galgad Empire had world domination in its sights, and Din had suffered countless casualties simply by virtue of sharing a border with an imperialist power.

After the war ended, little changed with regard to the Din Republic's pacifist national policies, but the country also began investing resources into spy education, hoping to turn the tides in the shadow war.

A decade later, there were spy training schools scattered across the nation.

Hundreds of headhunters scoured the country for promising children to send off to such institutions. From there, they whittled down the students' ranks mercilessly. In their eyes, nothing was worse than an incompetent spy. Every training academy held four grueling exams a year, and after each, the class would shrink. The graduation exams were so harsh that students even died taking them. And yet…

"Wait, I'm graduating? And I don't even have to take the exam? Hooraaaaay!"

…on that day, an exception was born.

The academy principal looked at the girl she'd called to her office and let out a large sigh.

"It's a *provisional* graduation. Not a graduation."

"But it means I can work as a full-fledged spy, right? Wow, and to think I was on the verge of flunking!"

"Yes, well…"

The principal examined the papers again, wondering why in the world the girl had been chosen.

Her alias was Lily, and she was seventeen years old. She did well on written tests and possessed an unusual physical idiosyncrasy, but her practical exam results were downright disastrous. She would make one huge blunder after another, then squeak in just over the passing line each time. Her homeroom teacher had been almost positive she would flunk out in her next exam.

The principal gave Lily another once-over. Perhaps she'd been picked for her looks alone. After all, she had luscious silver hair, an adorable baby face, and a voluptuous chest noticeable even beneath her clothes. Seventeen was obviously too young, but there were plenty of men who preferred girls her age. Maybe she had been chosen to lure men in and tempt them—in other words, as a honey trap.

"…Are you any good at seduction?"

"Huh? What? Whaaaaat? No way! I'm terrible with dirty stuff!"

"That's a pretty glaring weakness for a female spy…"

"Look, I don't know what you want me to say. Wait, you're not telling me that this mission I'm going on is…"

"I'm not."

Lily laid her hand on her chest in relief. "Oh, thank goodness."

The principal heaved another sigh.

Did they really know what they were getting into when they picked this girl?

"I'm not telling you that because I don't actually know the particulars." The principal glowered at Lily. "Do you know what an Impossible Mission is?"

Lily covered her mouth with her hand. "Uh, that's what they call a mission where somebody's already failed at it once, right?"

"That's right." The principal snapped her fingers. "An Impossible Mission is one that either has already been unsuccessfully attempted by another spy or soldier or is so difficult to begin with that it's been deemed impossible to complete."

"'Kay…"

"Now, I'm told they're putting together a team that specializes in these Impossible Missions."

"Huh?" Lily's eyes went wide.

The principal nodded in agreement. She thought it was just as unreasonable as Lily probably did.

When someone failed a mission, the difficulty of completing it on the second try went through the roof. Not only would the target be more wary, but any methods used the first time around would no longer be viable. And that wasn't even getting into all the information the failed attempt probably leaked.

Stay far away from Impossible Missions. In their world, that was just basic common sense.

Having a team that specialized in them was completely unheard-of.

"It's called Lamplight—and it's the team you've been assigned to."

Lily's expression froze.

The principal lowered her voice as she continued. "I'm going to be blunt here. You definitely have potential. You're exceptionally attractive, you have a useful ability inherent to your body, and you take your classes seriously. Your future holds promise."

"Hee-hee, it's been a while since anyone complimented me like that."

"But to put it another way, that's *all* you have going for you."

"…"

"The academy's official stance is that you're a washout on the verge of flunking. One of your teachers, a skilled educator who has nothing against you personally, deemed you 'unqualified to be a spy.' Personally, I find it difficult to imagine you accomplishing any of these hyper-difficult missions. Even for top-class operatives, less than one in ten Impossible Missions end in success, and they have a mortality rate of over ninety percent."

"Ninety percent...?"

"After hearing that, do you still want to join Lamplight?"

The principal's fears were well-founded. After all, Lily was a gigantic klutz.

In her test one month ago, she dropped her gun right in front of her target.

In her test four months ago, she got lost in the streets and only barely finished her objective on time.

And in her test seven months ago, she took the cipher she stole and accidentally flushed it down the toilet.

Each time, she had only passed by the narrowest of margins.

The principal felt a pang of guilt. Weren't they just sending this girl to her death?

"...You're saying that for my sake, aren't you?" Lily looked down. "Ha-ha; that's what makes it hurt so much to hear. Like a great big weight crushing my heart..."

"I don't want to see one of my students die."

However, that decision wasn't the principal's to make. Lily's assignment had come from a higher authority than the academy.

However, if Lily herself refused to go, then maybe, just maybe—

"I'll do it. I'll join Lamplight. And I swear I won't run away." The girl threw out her chest with pride. "Code name Flower Garden, ready to deploy and not afraid to die!"

Her eyes burned with resolve.

If that's true, thought the principal, *then I guess this will have to do.*

"Juuust kidding. I'm super-afraid of dying. ♪"

Lily stuck out her tongue.

She was at her dorm's incinerator and cheerfully talking to herself.

She tossed her personal effects into the furnace one after another, slowly but surely eliminating any trace that she had ever been enrolled there. As she watched the smoke rise over the mountain on which the academy was situated, she let out a proud *ahem*.

"It's basic deduction. If someone's assembling an elite team to take on Impossible Missions, then it's gonna be comprised of the best of the best. And that actually makes it *safer* than a regular old team. I've got it made! Man, I guess there's no point hiding talent as magnificent as mine. Heh, looks like game really does recognize game."

It was a well-known fact among the other students, but Lily's personality was really quite something.

Unconcerned by the principal's fears, she continued disposing of her things with nothing on her mind but glee at her provisional graduation.

I'm gonna be on an elite team!

Plus, the pay is awesome!

Just thinking about it had Lily downright ecstatic. "Whoo-hoo! Goodbye forever, childhood!" she cried as she tossed her old notebooks and test sheets into the fire. She had lived in the same dorm room for the past eight years, so there was quite a bit to get rid of.

Just as she was preparing to empty the last of her garbage can, a sheet of paper inside caught her eye.

"*Considering how much potential she shows and how low our current student count is, we've decided to pass her.*"

It was a report card, stuffed away in the very bottom of the bin.

She ripped it up without a word and tossed it into the incinerator.

All in all, there were ten forms that essentially said the same thing, and she did the same for each of them.

She had so much *potential*. That was the word they kept using to describe her. She was blessed with natural talents, and that was what had allowed her to remain at the academy for as long as she had. But when exactly were those talents supposed to bloom?

How many years of mediocrity would she have to suffer?

How many times would she have to endure the disdain of others?

"Screw that. I'm gonna do this." Lily was determined to burn away all the anguish the academy had put her through. "This lily's gonna join that elite team and come into full bloom there. See you never, alma mater!"

After cleaning out her dorm room, she immediately left. Sadly, she didn't have time to say good-bye to her classmates. When they saw her empty room, they would no doubt all come to the same conclusion. *Ah,* they'd say, *looks like the numbskull finally flunked out.*

Lily boarded an unfamiliar bus, then transferred to an overnight train.

The next day, she arrived in a port city—the third largest metropolis in the Din Republic. Between its proximity to the capital and its harbor serving as a gateway to the rest of the world, the city was bustling and prosperous. When Lily got off the train, she couldn't help but let out a sigh of amazement at the tightly packed lines of brickwork buildings.

She then set off down the road, sidestepping newsies and flower sellers as she headed to the specified establishment.

Her destination was a two-story building sandwiched between a watch store and a paint shop that sat on a road packed with white-collar workers coming and going. The sign outside read GARMOUTH SEMINARY, and there was a man smoking inside at what looked to be the front desk. Lily summoned her courage, then went in. "I'm the wonderful new transfer student," she declared.

The man gave her a short look, then gestured farther inside with his thumb. "In the back."

Ooh, this totally feels like spy stuff, Lily silently cooed.

On paper, Lily's cover was that she was a student at a fictitious seminary school. She'd even been sent a uniform and all the proper ID.

The room the receptionist had directed her to was a storeroom filled with piles of wooden crates. Upon sliding them aside, she discovered a stairway leading to an underground passage. The passage didn't have much in the way of light, but after following it for a short while, she reached an aboveground clearing.

And in the center, there was a massive manor.

In fact, the word *manor* hardly even seemed adequate. It was practically a palace, like the kind that nobles lived in.

Lily stared at it with her mouth agape.

How had she failed to notice something so ginormous? The answer to that lay in the city's buildings. They were so compressed that they were essentially ramparts completely blocking the manor from view.

There were probably people who'd lived in the city their whole lives who didn't even realize it existed.

So this is where the Lamplight members are... Lily swallowed. *Well, for an elite team that takes on Impossible Missions, their base definitely looks the part.*

Who knew what sorts of geniuses she would find inside?

Lily would be lying if she said she wasn't a bit scared, but more than anything, she hoped they were just as outstanding as she expected them to be. After all, she was counting on them to help awaken whatever talents she had hidden inside her.

She tried to suppress her heart's rapid thumping as she opened the manor's front door.

"Code name Flower Garden, at your service!"

As she did, she gave a bold, decidedly un-spy-like introduction.

Now, come on out, elites! Let's see what we're working with!

She looked inside, her eyes gleaming with nervousness and hope.

"Huh...?"

Then she cocked her head to the side.

In the foyer, there were six girls about the same age as her.

Laden with bags and suitcases, the young women turned to look at the new guest. It appeared they had just arrived as well, and all were wearing uniforms identical to the one Lily had been given.

One of the gaggle, a girl with short white hair, gave her a glare.

"Hey. You."

She had a commanding presence and keen, confident eyes. Her gaze was so pointed it felt like a knife. Between that and her lean, toned figure, she was really quite intimidating.

"What were your grades like?"

"Uh...does anyone know where all the Lamplight members are?"

"Answer the question. And no bullshit."

Whoa, what's with this sudden interrogation? Am I being tested?

Under the weight of the girl's menacing gaze, Lily reflexively blurted out the truth. "W-well, to be honest, I was pretty close to failing my—"

The rest of her answer was cut off by the ominous tolling of a clock filling the foyer.

There was a grandfather clock installed right in front of them, loud enough to reverberate through the whole manor.

When Lily looked, she discovered that it was six o'clock—the time she'd been instructed to arrive.

"Magnificent."

The seven girls looked up as one.

None of them had noticed when, but a suited figure had appeared atop the central staircase in the middle of the foyer.

At first glance, the person's fair complexion and shoulder-length hair suggested a woman, but upon further inspection of the slender frame devoid of any excess fat, it was just barely possible to identify the figure as a man—and a beautiful man at that.

However, the girls quickly realized that such beauty was the result of a systematic removal of anything wasteful or unnecessary, and there was something unsettling both about that fact and his expressionless, almost frozen-looking face. That said, as long as he did something about his hair, he'd be able to seamlessly disappear into any crowd in the city.

For some reason, though, his suit was stained a dark red. As if he'd just finished murdering someone.

"Welcome to Heat Haze Palace. I'm Klaus, the boss here at Lamplight."

Apparently, that was the name of this building.

The man continued his explanation from atop the stairs. "I'm glad to see you all made it. Myself and the seven of you make up the full ranks of Lamplight, and together, our job is to take on an Impossible Mission."

"Say what?" Lily replied.

"The mission begins in one month. Until then, I had planned to thoroughly train you, but…I imagine you're all tired from your journeys. We'll leave the training for tomorrow, and you can take today to get to know one another."

Klaus twirled around and headed back into the manor.

In his wake, he left a dumbfounded silence.

Sorry, *what* did he just say?

Was Lamplight really just one guy and a bunch of young girls?

Did they really have only one month until the Impossible Mission?

"The hell's that guy playing at?"

The commanding white-haired girl from before spoke again.

"I mean, rounding up a bunch of problem children to take on Impossible Missions? What gives?"

Lily's eyes went wide when she heard that worrying morsel of information.

The white-haired girl nodded solemnly. "Yeah, you heard that right. The seven of us? We're all washouts."

Lily was so taken aback by it all that she couldn't find anything to say.

The seven of them were just a group of young women.

Yet, they were going to work with a mysterious man they knew nothing about and take on an Impossible Mission.

The kind of mission so difficult it had a mortality rate of 90 percent.

Klaus had left without actually explaining anything, so the girls took it upon themselves to investigate the manor.

Even at a glance, it was clear how luxuriously Heat Haze Palace was decorated.

The entire building was carpeted in a lush red, and the lounge boasted an impressive selection of leather couches. Over in the kitchen, the cupboards were packed full of high-end tableware, and the gas-powered stove was state of the art. Down in the basement, there was even a rec room and a large communal bath.

Finally, their tour ended at the main hall. There, they found a message waiting for them.

A large blackboard was affixed to the wall and covered in text. Its letters were rounded, as though written by a woman's hand. The girls found it difficult to imagine Klaus having written them.

Heat Haze Palace Communal Living Rules

On the blackboard, a set of house rules were outlined in painstaking detail.

Lily let out a cry of delight. "Wait, we really get to live here?"

The other girls were equally excited.

Most of the rules laid out which rooms they were permitted in and ways to enter and exit the manor. That was all well and good. But when the girls got to the last two rules, they were a bit confused. Those two—just those two—were written in a much messier scrawl.

Rule ㉖: Work as seven to live together.

Rule ㉗: Give it your all when you're out and about.

Little question marks practically popped up over their heads.

The first of the addendums seemed almost childish, and the second didn't make any sense at all.

They puzzled over them, but no answer seemed forthcoming.

That was when the white-haired girl discovered an envelope on the table. "Hey, found some cash. Anyone else feel like throwing ourselves a welcoming party?"

Inside the envelope was money for their living expenses—and quite a bit of it.

Wanting to celebrate the occasion, the seven started preparing dinner. After going out and buying ingredients as a group, each of them got to work making a different dish. The manor's cooking utensils were top-shelf. And they weren't new, either; all had been well used.

The girls had been trained as spies, so they were reasonably proficient at housework. Dinner was ready in what seemed like no time at all.

Once the food was ready, they toasted with cups of apple juice, then began freely chatting among themselves.

It didn't take long for things to get rolling.

Whenever one of them would talk about how harsh her spy academy had been, another one would clap sympathetically, and a third would chime in with a masochistic grin and a story about how hers had been even worse. Then the cycle would repeat, and the conversation would proceed with nary an awkward pause or silence.

Maybe it's 'cause we're all washouts, Lily mused.

Not everyone would admit to her poor grades, but they'd all definitely had a rough time of it.

Though they came from a myriad of different schools and backgrounds and their ages were similarly varied, the girls were soon thick as thieves nonetheless.

Plus, meeting one another wasn't the only thing they had to be excited about—there was also the beautiful manor. Rules at the spy academies were strict, so it had been a while since any of them had been able to enjoy a meal in such a relaxed environment. Not to mention the food quality. Most of the meals served at the spy academies were meager, composed of little more than vegetable scraps and hunks of animal that were more gristle than meat.

"You know, back at my academy"—Lily took a big gulp of her juice—"I never realized that spies had it so nice. This isn't how I pictured them living at all."

"Right?! Feels like we're gonna be in heaven!"

The white-haired girl had a dreamy smile. During the conversation, Lily had learned that she was seventeen, just like her.

The two of them, now fast friends, exchanged a high five. ""Hooray!""

However, one of the other girls was scruntinizing their situation through much cooler eyes.

"It's weird."

Her hair was brown and permed, and her face had a decidedly timid look to it. She was also on the younger side at a mere fifteen. She fiddled her fingers restlessly with her head hanging down and her eyebrows drawn together. All in all, she gave off the impression of a small animal cowering in the face of a predator. Her eyes were moist, like she was on the verge of tears.

"Up until recently, there were definitely people living here."

"So?" replied the white-haired girl. "What's wrong with the place havin' a bit of history?"

"But…where'd they go? And also, what's up with this team? How are a bunch of underachievers like us supposed to handle an Impossible Mission?"

"Hmm? Well yeah, sure, I'm curious about all that, but I bet that guy'll explain everything tomorrow." The white-haired girl took another big bite of chicken. That was her way of saying that she was done talking about it.

However, the brown-haired girl seemed unsatisfied. She looked down despondently. "You're right; it is a bit different than I imagined."

That was when Lily spoke up. "So? This is pretty great, too, isn't it?"

The other girls all turned to her.

Lily gazed up at the chandelier hanging from the ceiling and went on warmly.

"I mean, just picture it. Living in a beautiful building, having three meals together every day, training and going out on missions, taking baths, eating meals, playing board games, enjoying the city's nightlife every now and again, becoming master spies... Doesn't that sound amazing?"

"You trying to sneak a fourth meal in there?" the white-haired girl quipped.

"Well, not *every* day."

"You're right, though; that doesn't sound half bad."

Nobody spoke up to disagree. In fact, they had probably all been thinking the same thing.

Then another girl cut in.

"Well, we know what we have to do to make that a reality."

She had straight-black hair, and at eighteen, she was the oldest of the group. Her exceptional figure seemed almost designed to draw gazes, her face was dazzlingly beautiful, and her elegant smile only served to accentuate her attractiveness.

"We have to clear that mission—together!" she declared with a very chairwomanly energy, and that served to settle the matter.

That seemed as good a moment as any to end the dinner.

After using rock-paper-scissors to decide who would have to clean up, the girls headed to their rooms. Heat Haze Palace had plenty of space to go around, so each of them had a bedroom all to herself.

What a nice group, Lily thought in satisfaction as she made for her room. On her way there, she spotted one of the other girls with a downcast expression.

It was the timid, brown-haired girl who had just been expressing her concerns.

"Still worried, huh?"

Lily flashed her a smile, and her new comrade gave a nod in return.

"I know it's lame, but yeah...," she replied in a quiet voice. The muscles in her face were tense. "Say, Lily, do you have anywhere you can escape to?"

"What do you mean?"

"Before the Impossible Mission starts, I'm going to run away."

"Hmm... Sorry, but I don't have a lot in the way of relatives. Actually, I don't have any family at all."

"Oh no... And with the provisional graduation, I can't even go back to my academy... I'm all out of options..."

Apparently, Lily's new friend didn't have any family, either.

Many of the spy academy students were orphans who'd lost both parents to accidents or disease.

Without some situation like that to force their hand, it was rare to find anyone willing to take on the grueling training of spy work.

"I wouldn't worry so much." Lily put on her broadest smile to cheer up her new teammate. "Think about it. That Klaus guy wouldn't gather a bunch of washouts without having some sort of plan, would he? If his team blows it, he's the one who's gonna be in danger. He probably has a bunch of brilliant lessons planned to hone our skills."

"A-and that'll make us strong enough to do Impossible Missions...?"

"Of course! I mean, that guy practically had an aura crackling around him. An aura that said *I'm gonna give you awesome lessons to awaken the talents sleeping within all of you!*"

Lily wasn't just saying that to console the brown-haired girl, either.

The sheer power emanating from that man put her spy academy teachers to shame. He was probably some sort of super-genius when it came to education. After all, it would have required supreme confidence to assemble a team of washouts to take on an Impossible Mission.

"...Yeah, I guess you're right." The brown-haired girl's expression softened. "Thank you. I feel a lot better. I should be able to get a good night's sleep now."

"Any time. Better get that shut-eye so you're ready for tomorrow's training!"

Lily gave her a small wave.

Obviously, she was worried, too. Without some unbelievably efficient help, they had no hope of taking on the Impossible Mission. She didn't have the mission's details yet, but with a bunch of washouts on one side and a 90 percent mortality rate on the other, the math was clear.

That was why she chose to believe in Klaus—and believe he had a plan.

The next morning marked their second day at Heat Haze Palace.

When the girls assembled in the main hall, Klaus made his appearance. Unlike yesterday's outfit stained in red, though, his suit and trousers this time were nice and clean. Lily found herself utterly captivated by his trim appearance.

She decided to greet him in an attempt to hide her racing heart. "Good morning, Boss."

"Oh, I don't like that at all." Klaus frowned. "Let's not call me Boss. Teach, maybe. Or just Klaus."

"Uh...okay. Teach it is, then."

"Fine by me. Now, let's get this Lamplight meeting started."

The couches in the main hall were arranged in a U-shape, and the girls had been sitting on them as they waited. They steeled themselves.

Klaus, completely unaffected by the tension in the room, began speaking leisurely.

"Allow me to explain. Lamplight is a provisional team built to take on an Impossible Mission, one that revolves around infiltrating a laboratory in the Galgad Empire. I'll get into the particulars at a later date, but our task is to steal something from inside it. The reason it's been designated an Impossible Mission is because a team of our operatives failed to complete it last month. There were no survivors, and we received no intel back from them."

"No survivors...," one of the girls murmured.

Klaus nodded. "We depart for the infiltration mission in one month. That doesn't give us much time."

Even though she'd heard this before, Lily felt a chill run up her legs.

They were a bunch of washouts, and yet, they were supposed to take on a mission that a group of expert spies had failed at. It all felt like some kind of sick joke.

"But don't worry." Klaus's voice grew gentler. "As you can see, I'm *the Greatest Spy in the World*. There isn't a spy alive who's better than me. Once you've taken my lessons, Impossible Missions will be like child's play to you."

The man clearly had confidence in his educational skills.

From the way he was acting, it was like he wasn't scared of anything.

"Dunno how I'm supposed to 'see' that," the white-haired girl retorted coldly, unimpressed by Klaus's bold statement.

Klaus gave her a big nod. "Why not decide for yourself after taking this lesson, then?"

He drew a set of padlocks from the hall's wooden box, then tossed one to each recruit.

"This is the model of lock the Empire formerly used at their military facilities. Being able to pick them is an essential skill for infiltration work."

Lily inspected the padlock she'd been given. It was a good deal bulkier and heavier than the kind in common circulation.

"Now, open it. You have one minute."

A pop quiz!

With no time to even think, Lily reached into her pocket and withdrew her lock-picking tool. However, the instant she inserted it into the mechanism, she could tell just how doomed she was. The padlock was custom-made and came equipped with anti-picking features. She couldn't even tell where the shear line was obstructed.

How am I supposed to get this done in one minute?! Lily lamented.

She gave it her best shot, but the minute was up before she knew it.

"That's time," Klaus called.

Lily looked around and discovered that only one of her compatriots had proven successful. The other six had failed spectacularly.

However, that was to be expected.

Even at her spy academy, Lily had never seen such a complex padlock before.

Klaus came around and retrieved the unopened locks.

"Only one success? Well, don't worry. That was more or less what I expected."

"Rgh…" The white-haired girl's face flushed scarlet. "What, and you can do better?"

"See for yourself."

The next moment, Klaus tossed his six padlocks into the air.

"You just go like this…and they open pleasantly."

Lily couldn't even follow what happened next.

Klaus had swung his arm two or three times, that much she was sure of.

However, she hadn't been able to make out anything else. All she could see was the end result.

Six perfectly unclasped padlocks resting on the carpet.

Forget one minute apiece—he'd done six of them in the span of a second.

"Whoa…," one of the girls murmured.

Lily just gawked in blank shock.

This man was on a completely different level than her teachers back at the academy. With skills like these, he could stroll into any facility in the world and steal whatever confidential documents he pleased. The unbelievable feat she'd just witnessed had left her certain of that.

So *that* was the power of an active-duty spy…

Hell, it bordered on superhuman.

"I told you, didn't I? There isn't a spy alive who's better than me."

Now it was clear—he had the raw skills to back up that confidence of his.

Lily's legs weren't trembling anymore.

This was a man she could believe in.

"After seeing that, do any of you still have doubts?"

The girls shook their heads in unison. Not one spoke up in dissent. Now the lot of them were staring at Klaus, their eyes gleaming with envy and hope.

Their expressions screamed one thing: *We want to take this man's lessons ASAP.*

And as for Lily, her eyes were wide with anticipation. Maybe he really could change her.

Under the weight of his students' envious gazes, Klaus calmly proceeded. "Now, moving on to the next lecture…"

"What?"

"Yes?"

A strange pause filled the air.

Klaus tilted his head in confusion, and Lily let out a bewildered "Huh?"

She must have been imagining things. What an odd thing for her teacher to say.

Realizing her mistake, Lily bowed to Klaus. "Sorry, Teach. I know I shouldn't interrupt."

"No, no. If you have a question, then by all means, ask it."

"Nope, no questions here! Please go on with the explanation. I'm dying to hear the rest of—"

"That *was* the explanation."

"Pardon...?"

"If you use your picklock pleasantly, the lock will open. You were using them unpleasantly, so they didn't. That concludes the lesson on lock picking."

《《《《《《《《　　　　　　　》》》》》》》》
....

A heavy communal silence descended upon the girls. They shot glances at one another. Sure enough, they were all thinking the same thing.

Was that man, by any chance...?

Klaus could clearly sense that something was up. He looked back at them, bewildered. "...Don't tell me you had trouble understanding that?"

The phrase *Don't tell me* seemed ironic coming from a man whose lesson hadn't told *them* anything.

Lily returned his gaze with the full depth of that sentiment burning in her eyes.

Klaus crossed his arms, then sank into silence for a moment before finally speaking again. "...How about this? As a special favor, I'll go over my plans for the syllabus. First off is the 'talk beautifully' negotiation unit, followed by the 'just take them down' combat unit, and after that, the 'it'll all work out' unit on disguises. Do you think you'll be able to follow that?"

"Nope."

"Really?"

"Really."

"What if I changed the 'talk beautifully' part to 'talk like a butterfly'?"

"That...makes it worse."

"I see. Magnificent." Klaus nodded deeply, then exhaled at length. "I'm just realizing this now, but...it would appear I'm quite bad at teaching."

After casually making that outrageous observation, he strode across the main hall. He passed in front of the girls gaping at him in shock, reached the door—

"The rest of the day will be self-study."

—and with that final comment, left the room.

You could hear a pin drop.

The girls were silent for a moment, but after what had just happened sank in, they exchanged glances, nodded, then stood as a unit—

""""""""HOLD UUUUUUUUP!""""""""

—and shouted as one.

The main hall was in abject chaos.

"What in the world did I just witness?!" "Does he think this is all a joke?!" "Okay, I really need to ask—what's so 'magnificent' about any of this?!" "That was awful…"

However, the girls could hardly be blamed for their animated ranting.

Their sole hope had just been lost to them. There was only one way a bunch of washouts could have cleared an Impossible Mission, and now, even that was gone.

"Now how are we supposed to complete that mission?!" The brown-haired girl looked even closer to tears than usual.

Lily's lip quivered as their situation finally began to sink in.

Lamplight's boss was unbelievably useless.

"W-well, even at worst, we can still train among ourselves and get stronger that way…"

"But training isn't the only issue here." The black-haired girl laid a finger against her face. The gesture gave her an elegant, mature air. "In addition to being our teacher, he's also our boss. That means we'll be acting under his command during our mission."

"Uh…so?"

"Will he be able to give us actual orders? I worry that he's more likely to tell us to *Sneak around the back pleasantly* and *Search the area like a mole*."

That was disturbingly plausible.

In fact, it seemed almost guaranteed to happen.

Lily could feel the color drain from her face.

This was a crisis the likes of which they'd never seen.

The white-haired girl summed things up nicely when she screamed, "WHAT THE HEEEEEEELL?!"

It was like a dam had opened, and the other girls began voicing their complaints at once.

In one fell swoop, they'd been dropped from heaven straight into hell.

And thus, the freshly minted spy team Lamplight fell apart less than a single hour into its existence.

Lily walked across the busy street with a bundle of groceries in her arms.

She had purchased them just fine, but now her legs felt like lumps of lead. Her gait was gloomy as she headed back to Heat Haze Palace, and as she nearly dropped the potatoes for the umpteenth time, she let out a heavy sigh.

How the heck did we end up here...?

After the meeting, Klaus had holed himself up in his room. He had yet to emerge.

Left with no other choice, the girls began practicing lock picking on their own, but that was no different than what they'd already been doing at their spy academies. No sudden bursts of insight seemed likely to come.

If self-study was all they needed to become strong, they wouldn't have been washouts in the first place.

There was no way they'd be able to clear next month's Impossible Mission.

And who exactly was the big dum-dum who went and talked a big game about how Teach would have a bunch of brilliant lessons planned to hone our skills?! Forget discovering my latent talent—at this rate, I'm gonna die!

As she silently cursed everything, Lily trembled at the all-too-real future looming before her.

Now that she thought about it, this was probably exactly what her principal had been worried about.

…Would it be better to just make a break for it?

She was reminded of something one of her teammates had suggested the day prior.

But there really isn't anywhere I can go… And besides—

—what would become of her teammates if she fled on her own?

What would become of the intimidating white-haired girl who had nodded, saying *"You're right, though; that doesn't sound half bad."*

What would become of the black-haired girl who had elegantly cheered them up by saying *"We have to clear that mission—together!"*

What would become of the brown-haired girl who had given her a timid smile as she said *"Thank you. I feel a lot better. I should be able to get a good night's sleep now."*

Lily had only known them for a single night.

However, they were all around her age and had all endured the same things she had. Could she really just leave them to die…?

But…what can I do?

In that moment, an idea sprang up in her mind—the one way she could break the deadlock.

She immediately dismissed it as impossible.

However, the plan she came up with refused to go away so easily. The longer she thought about it, the more convinced she became that it was her only option.

Then she heard something.

An old woman's voice emerged from the crowd. "Stop, thief!"

Lily whirled around.

A large man was running through the city's hustle and bustle with a purse clutched in his hand, pushing people aside as he made his escape. What's more, he was heading straight toward her.

He gave her a hard shove. "Outta my way, kid!"

His arms felt as thick as logs, and Lily collapsed by the roadside with an "Ah!"

Meanwhile, the man just kept running.

"Ow-ow-ow…"

Lily rubbed her bum, then began collecting her fallen potatoes. As she was counting them and blowing the dirt off, a genteel-looking old lady came up to her.

She must have been the purse snatcher's victim.

"Are you all right, young miss...?"

"Huh? Oh yeah, I'm fine."

The old woman's frail eyebrows turned downward. "It looks like today just isn't our day. At least we're still alive, though, eh?"

"Hmm... Yeah, you're right." Lily gave her a smile. "It's definitely good to be alive."

"Exactly."

"After all, you have to be alive to have a good dinner!"

"I like your positivity, miss."

"I mean, good grief! Here I am, worrying my brains out, and then *he* comes along with this trivial nonsense. If you ask me, he should be more grateful that *he* gets to be alive."

The old woman frowned. "Hmm? Who should be more grateful?"

"Isn't it obvious?" Lily gave her a small grin and pointed forward. "The purse snatcher."

Just ahead of them was the large man—collapsed on the ground.

The old woman didn't understand what had happened.

The purse snatcher had been making his getaway just a moment ago, but now he was unconscious and frothing at the mouth.

What had changed in the past few seconds?

"Looks like he probably has a chronic disease or something."

Lily headed over to the petty criminal and covertly withdrew a needle from his arm. Afterward, she retrieved the purse, then undid her hair ribbon and used it to tie him up. The police were already on their way, and they could handle the rest.

She looked down at the unconscious man and gave a small nod.

That's right... We're spies.

As she handed the bewildered old woman her purse back, Lily cheerfully asked her a question.

"By the way, ma'am, does this town have any tourist attractions?"

She had to do it. Her foe was powerful, but this was the only way to survive. Letting her resolve waver would do nothing but waste valuable time.

Silently and inwardly, Lily smiled.

She then murmured to herself in her heart of hearts.

If it's the only choice I've got...then I'll just have to take the target down.

As she did, she quietly steeled herself.

I'm code name Flower Garden—and it's time to bloom out of control.

Klaus's bedroom was at the far end of Heat Haze Palace's second story.

The manor had many delightfully lavish rooms to its name, but for some reason, Klaus didn't use any of them. Given the building's layout, his room couldn't possibly have been all that spacious. A very odd choice.

Maybe it's got some sort of secret passageway in it or something, Lily mused as she knocked on his door.

There was no answer.

She knocked and knocked but didn't get so much as a peep from inside.

When she gave up and just opened it, she immediately spotted Klaus. Perhaps he simply had a policy of ignoring knocking.

Inside, the room looked like a murder scene.

Lily let out a shriek when she saw the red liquid splattered everywhere. It was only a moment later, when the pungent smell of oil hit her nose, that she realized it was just paint and calmed down.

Klaus was sitting on a chair in front of a canvas with his arms crossed.

"What do you need?" He looked up. "As for me, well, it's as you can see."

"Wait, you're doing what?"

"Trying to come up with new teaching methods."

To her, it definitely just looked like he was painting.

However, there was also a decent stack of books piled up around his feet, all of which featured *pedagogy* and *education* in their titles. It appeared he was trying to learn by trial and error. What's more, he was actually taking it seriously.

Curious as to what role the oil painting played in all that, Lily gave it another look. The piece was abstract and made up entirely of violent red lines layered atop one another.

Down in the bottom right corner, she could see the word *Family*.

Was that its title? Was this dumping ground of paint supposed to represent family?

The man's thought processes defied comprehension.

"So does it look like you're gonna find any awesome new teaching techniques?"

His answer was immediate. "It does not."

Lily's shoulders slumped. Sure enough, the man was useless.

"Don't worry, though. I should have a firm answer within the week."

They couldn't afford to wait a week. The mission was only a month away, and it was getting closer every minute.

She gulped, then offered a suggestion.

"Y'know, Teach, I actually had an idea."

"What's that?"

"Let's get out of the house for a bit."

Klaus furrowed his brow. "To what end...?"

"For a change of pace!" Lily gave him a big nod. "When you stay cooped up in a small, little room, your ideas get small and cooped-up, too. That's when it's time to go for a walk! Putting your nose to the grindstone is good and all, but keeping your brain refreshed is just as important."

"But I already went on a walk. Last week."

"Oh well, I guess you're all set... Wait, you're missing the whole point!"

"I see you're quite taken with this idea." Klaus shook his head. "I do appreciate the concern...but I can't say I'm all that interested."

"But you just spent the whole day in here and couldn't think of anything, right?"

"Way to hit a man while he's down."

For a brief moment, Klaus narrowed his eyes.

Lily was afraid she'd made him mad, and her heart began racing. However, his expression changed no more than that. Perhaps he'd meant it to be a smile.

"C'mon, it'll be fun! I even went around town asking where all the famous spots are!"

"I see. And?"

"Oh-ho, I thought you'd never ask! I found all sorts of places. For instance, there's this Kotoko Museum that's got two-thousand-year-old artifacts on display. And there's a carnival!"

"Neither of those really speak to me. Anything else?"

"Huh? Uh...there's this road with lots of places to eat called Maple Lane; there's a beach that's supposedly haunted; there's a church with gorgeous stained-glass windows..."

Having failed to catch Klaus's attention on her first attempt, Lily began throwing out suggestions more or less at random.

"........."

After listening to her pitch, Klaus went silent for a bit—

"Magnificent."

—then crossed his arms in satisfaction.

"All right, I'm in. But it's already pretty late, so let's save the outing for tomorrow."

Lily glanced out the window. Sure enough, the sky had taken on a vivid shade of orange.

She would have preferred to go today, but this was fine, too. She couldn't afford to force the issue and risk offending Klaus right after she'd finally gotten him on board.

"All right! See you tomorrow!"

Lily flashed him her finest smile.

Step one, complete.

Although its name might have suggested otherwise, Maple Lane wasn't a mountain path surrounded by a thick forest of maple trees but a road smack-dab in the middle of the city. Its storefronts featured all sorts of delicacies and goods imported from abroad.

It was also one of the largest streets in the entire Din Republic, and while its shops were crowded at the best of times, holidays were something else entirely. The road was packed with food carts, and fragrant aromas wafted through the air. Between the herb-roasted lobsters and potatoes, the bacon and mushrooms sautéed in butter, and the walnut cakes, it seemed impossible to pick just one.

It was around noon on their third day at Heat Haze Palace, and Lily found herself overwhelmed by the splendor.

The street was teeming with smiling people. There were children sucking on lollipops and holding their parents' hands, couples with goofy grins listening to storefront radios, and old men sitting in front of a pocket watch shop and nodding along in fascination as they watched the craftsman work.

As she looked out at the prosperous market, Lily raised her voice.

"Woooow, I've never seen so many people in one place before! What a nightmare!"

"........."

"Sorry, that last part wasn't supposed to be out loud..."

"A mistake like that can easily prove fatal," Klaus pointed out. "By the way, where's the rest of the team? I had assumed some of them would be joining us."

"I asked, but they all said they wanted to focus on their independent training."

That was a lie. Lily had actually snuck out without saying anything.

The two of them headed down the street.

The plan was that they'd window-shop for a bit before taking a break at a restaurant famed for its wonderful shellfish.

On their way there, they found a cart selling tasty-looking canned food, so they bought some for later. The lobster and crab on display looked fantastic as well, but because they weren't planning on heading back to Heat Haze Palace immediately, they decided to just take note of the location for next time.

As Lily flitted from one food cart to the next, Klaus called over to her.

"Ah, that's right, you're from out in the country. I take it you didn't get many chances to visit the city."

"Yup, and my first practical exam in an urban area was a disaster. The ground on the streets was really hard, so I kept tripping and getting lost. I'm totally used to it now, though."

"Really? You seem awfully excited for someone who claims to be used to the city."

"No, I meant I'm used to getting lost."

"Ah, then it's no wonder."

Klaus nodded, then turned his body.

"The restaurant's this way."

Somehow, she had already made a wrong turn.

She could feel her face go red as she followed after Klaus.

"Teach, I've got a question." Lily raised a finger. "Could you teach me how we got here from the station?"

"Hmm? Well, we started by heading southwest, took a left at the post office, then a right by the funeral home, then followed the road for a while until eventually taking a left at the radio shop."

"Wow, you actually taught me!"

"Is there some reason I wouldn't? I led us on a bit of a detour because of the emergency construction work, but I can at least remember which streets we took."

"Huh, I don't remember seeing any signs about construction. How'd you realize it was going on?"

"I just did."

"………"

But that's the most important part!

However, Lily swallowed her words. Shouting at him wouldn't accomplish anything. "Was it by the pedestrian count, maybe? Like, you saw that the number of people passing by was different than usual or something like that?"

"Ah, now that you mention it, that might well have been it," he agreed readily.

It wasn't that he'd been hiding it from her; he just hadn't consciously realized it himself.

Lily groaned internally.

Why? Why did there have to be things he could teach just fine and things he couldn't teach at all?

But right as the question passed through her head—

"Ah!"

—Lily suddenly lost her footing.

"Help!" she cried.

There was a small dent in the cobblestone she hadn't noticed.

As she felt gravity begin to take her, she lost her grip on the four cans she was holding.

Before her jaw could smack into the ground, though, her body came to an abrupt stop.

"Are you all right?"

She turned her head to find that Klaus had caught her. His handsome face was right next to hers, and after she realized that...and after also realizing that her ample bosom was pressing right into his arm—

"Hyeep!"

—she leaped back.

It felt like her whole body was going to burn up.

Klaus, for his part, was as impossible to read as always. Upon further inspection, she discovered he was holding all the cans she'd lost control of in his other hand. Not only had he caught her, he also hadn't let a single one of them drop.

"W-wow, Teach. Teaching aside, you've got some mad skills..."

She had complimented him in an attempt to hide her embarrassment, but Klaus just shook his head. "That really wasn't anything deserving of praise." It was almost as though he was disappointed in her for commending him. "Oh, and by the way, I've identified the reason I can't explain things well."

"You have?"

Instead of replying to Lily's surprised question, Klaus took the cans and tossed them high in the air.

As they tumbled end over end toward Lily, she reached out with both hands and caught them. "What was that about?"

"How did you catch the cans?"

"Well, I kinda cupped my hands like a bowl—"

"And how did you move your legs?"

"........."

She didn't know how to answer that.

Legs? Did I move my legs just now?

Did she slide them to the spot where the cans would land? Did she bend them just a little when she made the catch? She got the feeling she had shifted her center of gravity over to her left leg for a moment, but she wasn't at all confident enough to say so.

The only answer she could really give was...

"...I just kind of did."

"And that's how I feel," Klaus said. "You can explain that you caught the cans, but you can't explain every tiny step you took in the process."

"This has to be a joke," Lily murmured.

Looking at his eyes, though, she could tell he was dead serious.

In short, the problem was that they had a huge gap—the gap between his intuition and theirs.

Could a person really explain how to grip an object? How to get out of a bed? How to take off a shirt?

Klaus was the exact same way, only about how to pick locks, how to disguise oneself, and how to fight.

But if that was true, then that would mean he was on a whole other...

Lily gulped. "But then, how are you ever supposed to teach us?"

"That's what I'm racking my brain to figure out."

His answer was as dispassionate as ever, but she could hear a whisper of fatigue lurking in his voice.

She thought back to the mountain of books in his room. He definitely wasn't slacking off.

He was giving the matter his earnest, sincere, and serious consideration, yet he still couldn't come up with a solution.

"........."

Lily closed her eyes for a moment.

Then, she reopened them and struck a triumphant pose. "Aha! But you're forgetting why we came here in the first place!"

"How so?"

"We're here to decompress! To leave all our pesky problems behind and get our heads nice and empty!"

"Are you familiar with the word *capricious*?"

"Hee-hee. Back at the academy, they called me the girl you'd hate to have as an enemy or a friend!"

"Ah, so they treated you like a weirdo? I'm sorry to hear that."

"I bet you'd know all about that!"

As they shared their slightly offbeat conversation, they continued walking past rows of food carts.

Suddenly, a scenic picture in one of the storefronts caught Lily's eye. "Teach, check it out!"

She grabbed Klaus's sleeve and tugged him to a stop.

The image she found was a landscape photograph hanging off of a juice vendor's cart. It depicted a lake surrounded by lush natural scenery. The photo was black-and-white, but even that was enough to convey the vivid beauty of the setting.

"It's so pretty..."

"Oh, the Emai Lake photo?" The shopkeeper cheerfully launched into an explanation. "Y'know, if you head to the station and take the public bus, you can get there in just a little over two hours. 'Course, today's a holiday, so it's going to be pretty packed."

"Wow, it sounds really popular!"

"Popular? That place is the biggest tourist attraction around. Hotshots from the capital like to get together and go there for their R & R. It's real nice. There's even boats available to rent."

Lily bought a bottle of juice to thank the vendor for the info, then turned to Klaus and chuckled. "Hee-hee, looks like we got ourselves a juicy bit of intel. We should head there later."

"...Very well, then."

Not only had Klaus agreed, he hadn't even sounded displeased or anything. Maybe, just maybe, he was starting to enjoy himself a little.

Step two, complete.

After eating at the restaurant, the two of them headed for Emai Lake.

They were told it would take two hours to get there by bus, but in Klaus's car, it only took half that. Contrary to what Lily had expected, his car was the type of boring old black passenger car you could find just about anywhere. When she pointed that fact out, though, he replied by, quite reasonably, asking her, "What kind of spy actively attracts attention?" It was a perfectly valid point, which felt all the more unreasonable coming from an oddball like him.

Just as the juice vendor warned, the lake was swarming with tourists, all packed together as they carried parasols and sipped fancy cocktails.

The pair headed to the lakeshore and found a large sign describing the lake.

According to the sign, the lake was huge, at almost half a square mile, and the surrounding mountains blessed it with a bounty of natural splendor. By borrowing a boat and rowing to its center, the sign promised you could admire Mother Nature in blissful tranquility.

Perhaps because of the lack of wind, the lake reflected the sun's light like a vast mirror. Enjoying such a beautiful sight from a rowboat would be a wonderfully sophisticated experience.

"Given how crowded it is, I don't imagine there will be any boats available," Klaus remarked.

"It's fine; we'll just wait for one to come back."

Even though they were prepared to wait, when they eventually made it to the dock, they were fortunate enough to find one rowboat still there—a small two-seater.

"Ooh, looks like it's our lucky day."

"By the way…I suppose I'm the one rowing?"

"Well, you *are* the guy…"

"I suppose I am," Klaus replied, stepping in ahead of her. Once he was aboard, he offered her his hand.

Nervously, Lily took it and boarded as well.

His hand was surprisingly warm.

Once they set off, the boat reached the middle of the lake in no time at all. Even Klaus's rowing skills were top-notch. "You're so fast!" Lily praised him, to which she received yet another enigmatic reply.

"I'm just rowing like a cloud."

Around that time, the sun began setting, painting the sky red and dyeing the lake, its shore, and the trees dotting the mountains the color of sunset. From out there, the people on the lakeshore looked like tiny orange specks.

They couldn't hear the city's hustle and bustle, and there were no boats nearby to break the silence, either.

The only inhabitants of that fiery orange world were Lily and Klaus.

"It's so much prettier than the picture, isn't it?"

"That it is."

Apparently, it failed to warrant a "magnificent." Perhaps he had some sort of internal rating scale he used.

"Lily."

"Ah, y-yeah? Y'know, that's the first time I've heard you call me by my name."

"Never forget the things you saw today or the scenery you're looking at now."

Klaus turned his black eyes toward the people on the shore.

"Never forget the smiles of the children playing on the streets. Never forget the natural views so beautiful you want to embrace them in your arms. Never forget those precious people basking in the evening glow."

"Huh…"

"Twelve years ago, the Empire invaded. We had declared neutrality, but they didn't care. Our people were powerless to resist their aggression, and they were massacred. And now, ten years after the carnage, the Empire is invading again as part of the shadow war."

"Wait, they are?"

"That market we were in might have seemed peaceful, but a bomb once very nearly went off in it. The perpetrator was an Imperial spy trying to assassinate a key member of our Ministry of Foreign Affairs. The person who found out and put a stop to it was an operative who specialized in intelligence work. It wasn't a police officer, it wasn't a soldier, it wasn't a bureaucrat, and it wasn't a politician."

Klaus continued.

"The world is awash in pain. Spies like us are the only ones who can stop these tragedies from occurring." To drive the point home, he said, "Never forget that."

Then, seemingly satisfied, he returned to gazing at the sunset.

"……………"

The sentiment behind his words was full of fire, but Lily filled her heart with ice to resist them.

They may have been gazing at the same view, but the two of them were simply too different.

He had no idea what it was like to be her.

He probably couldn't even imagine how disheartening that speech had been for her.

"…But if I die, then it'll all have been for nothing," she replied. "Sure, I love my homeland, and sure, I get how important this mission is. I almost died in the war, and it was a spy who saved me at the last minute. That's why I wanna become a good spy, and it's why I look up to you guys. But at the same time…it's also why I can't just risk throwing my life away."

Partway through, she cast her gaze downward, unable to look Klaus in the eye anymore.

"I want to come into bloom someday, y'know?"

"………"

"Maybe I feel this way 'cause I'm a washout, but… After surviving a war, putting up with contempt from everyone at school, and then finally lucking out and becoming a spy, if I just end up dying for nothing, then what was the point of it all?"

But you probably don't understand this feeling, this coldness that chills me down to my very core. You and I are too different.

Lily sighed, then clenched her fist in front of her chest.

"Teach…"

"Yes?"

"The wind's too cold. Is it okay if I sit closer to you…?"

"The wind isn't blowing, though."

"Girls get cold easier." Lily sat up and headed over to Klaus.

The boat wobbled as its center of gravity shifted.

"I figured it out, you know. Why you brought together a bunch of washouts. We're sacrifices for another scheme, aren't we?"

That was the only possible explanation she'd been able to come up with. The only good reason to put a bunch of failing students together with a teacher who couldn't teach.

She was impressed at how logical it was.

Sending her and the others in to die on a high-mortality mission would gather all sorts of useful intel, and because they were all washouts with no future anyway, the cost of doing so was relatively low. Then, a group of competent spies could go in later and use whatever information the girls had gathered to complete the mission with flying colors.

Lily laid her hand on Klaus's knee.

She leaned in so close their faces were almost touching.

"I spent all day today watching you, and now I'm certain. You can't teach. And we're just here to die. But I don't want that. Because someday, once I come into my own, I want to be able to look back and smile. And I'm willing to do whatever it takes to get to that point—and that means not dying here."

"Lily…?"

"I'm sorry, Teach. I really, really am."

She looked Klaus right in the eye.

"I'm code name Flower Garden—and it's time to bloom out of control."

That's when it happened.

A burst of poison gas sprayed up from her chest.

Twelve years ago, during the Galgad Empire's invasion, they made use of one particularly inhumane weapon. It was extremely lethal, didn't leave behind evidence the way a bomb did, and remained in place and unseen for long periods of time—poison gas.

Wanting to test its effectiveness, they decided to unleash it on a small village in the Din Republic. In an instant, the once-happy village became hell on earth, and the hundreds of people living there all perished in the blink of an eye.

A spy sent word of the incident to the military, and when the soldiers came running, they found something there.

A young girl on death's door, who had a very unique physical trait...

Klaus had no time to react before the gas struck him.

Even if he'd seen it coming, he wouldn't have been able to escape it anyway. Not only had the attack been launched from point-blank range, but also Lily was holding down his leg. As far as she could tell, the gas from her chest had nailed him straight in the nose and mouth.

With a dumbfounded look on his face, he shoved Lily away.

However, it was too late. Her plan had already worked.

"Paralytic...gas...?"

He was clearly having trouble speaking.

After looking at his trembling fingers, he hurriedly made to cover his mouth. He only twitched and toppled to the side, unable to even sit up anymore.

"This doesn't make sense... Spraying gas at this range is just suicide..."

"Except this poison doesn't work on me."

"…How do you mean?"

"My body's got what they call a special trait." Lily smiled like there was nothing to it.

Despite being surrounded by poison gas strong enough to render an adult male immobile, she was cool as a cucumber.

"So? Not even you can resist poison, right?"

The lake's wind had dispersed the rest of the gas, but it had lingered long enough to lay Klaus low.

Still on his side, his body continued twitching.

Lily was so pleased with herself, she had to laugh. "Ah-ha-ha! I guess fooling an elite spy is easier than I expected, huh?"

Klaus jerked some more, his face pale. The poison had left him almost entirely incapacitated.

To get to this point, Lily had had to weave plans within plans.

First, she had to invite him out under the pretext of wanting to give him a change of pace, then she had to maneuver them both onto a rented boat while making it seem spontaneous. In the end, though, she managed to pull off her sneak attack perfectly without ever once uttering the word *lake*.

Not even an elite spy like him could break out of the trap she'd engineered. Victory was hers.

"Hee-hee. You feel coerced yet, Teach?"

"Don't…screw with me…" Klaus glared at her. "What are you even after…?"

"I want you to make me a promise."

"If you don't need it in writing, I'm happy to say whatever you want me to."

"C'mon, don't give me that lip. I know my poisons are good, y'know," she replied with sickening sweetness as she drew a new weapon from her pocket.

It was a needle, dripping with purple liquid.

"This poison's a special concoction of mine. One prick, and even a grown man goes out like a light."

"………"

"If you try to go against me, I *will* stab you."

That was her way of ensuring he made good on his promise.

She brought the needle close to Klaus's face. It was the same quick-acting poison she had used the day before to take down the purse snatcher.

Despite the peril literally before his eyes, Klaus didn't move. Or rather, he couldn't.

Lily gave him a smile. "I have two demands. First, I want Lamplight disbanded. And second, I want you to guarantee its members' livelihoods."

"………"

"I just don't want us to die—especially not at the hands of a teacher who can't even teach."

Given the man's skills, he must have had money and connections he could throw around at will. Using those was their only chance of surviving.

Klaus stared at her menacingly. "That's enough joking around. If you come any closer, I will fight back."

"Please, there's no need to bluff. We both know you can't move under the poison. And you don't have any weapons anyway, right?"

"How do you…?"

"I checked. Earlier, when you caught me."

His hollow threats wouldn't work on her. She had prepared for that, too.

Klaus's eyes went wide. "So you tripping back at Maple Lane was just an act?"

"Uhhhh…*yeah*, that was definitely all part of my plan…"

It was not. Her original plan to check him for weapons had been something else entirely.

"A-anyway! Teach, if you know what's good for you, you'll do what I say."

Lily proudly threw out her chest and inched the needle ever closer to Klaus's motionless body.

She had used every ounce of talent she had and all the skills she'd been polishing, but she had taken down an elite operative all on her own.

It was over.

"…Looks like you have all your bases covered."

At long last, her target stopped resisting.

With a large sigh, he gave her a look filled with resignation.

"The paralytic ran through me in moments, and all I can move are my tongue and my feet. That means swimming isn't an option. I could try calling for help, but we're in the middle of a lake. And I'm dealing with a trained apprentice spy, so hoping to randomly find a weapon I can use in this rented boat is a nonstarter as well. It would appear that this truly is—"

"—Checkout."

"Checkmate, indeed."

Fortunately, Klaus didn't point out that she'd bungled her cool one-liner.

"There is one thing I don't know, though," he went on.

"…Hmm? It seems a bit late to be asking questions, but what?"

"Something that's been bugging me for some time."

"Like I said, what?"

"Lily, I have to ask…"

He gave her a profound look.

"…how much longer should I keep playing along with your game?"

As he spoke, two changes took place.

"Huh?"

One was on Lily's right ankle. All of a sudden, she discovered a large shackle around it.

The other was at the bottom of the boat. When she looked down, she found it was slowly taking on water.

What in the…? she thought as she took in the situation. Klaus was stretching his left leg out as far as he could. Apparently, the miniscule motion of which he was still capable had been enough to activate his trap.

"Wh-what's going on?"

"I used my special-made shackle. I also unstoppered the boat."

"There was a stopper…?"

"In eight minutes, this boat is going to sink. And because you're chained to it, so will you."

Realization hit Lily like a bolt of electricity.

Sure enough, there was a chain attaching the shackle around her ankle to the boat. It must have been hidden under one of the seats, because this was her first time seeing it.

She pulled out her picking tool and slid it into the shackle's lock, but she couldn't get it to budge. In fact, she couldn't even figure out what kind of lock it was. After giving up on opening it, she moved on to trying to break the chain. However, it was made of thick iron, so she had no luck there, either.

"You're not getting out of it," Klaus told her. "The key isn't on the boat, and with your skills, you'll never get the shackle open. No matter what you do, you're going down with the boat."

"That's horrible..."

"Unless I open it for you, that is."

".........!"

"Give me the antidote. That's my one condition."

Lily bit her lip. So that was what he was after.

However, she wasn't ready to admit defeat just yet.

"B-but...this doesn't change anything! Open the lock, or I'll stab you with my—"

"Your needle? Go ahead."

"Huh...?"

"It'll knock me out, right? But if I'm knocked out, how do you intend to get that shackle off?"

"*Gulp...*"

This time, Lily went quiet. She was out of options.

In fact, she'd been completely routed.

Meanwhile, the boat was still taking on water. Both she and it were slowly sinking.

This wasn't right—*she* was the one who was supposed to win.

"But...how?"

"Hmm?"

She began moaning and complaining like a child. "I never told anyone! I didn't tell a single person I was laying a trap for you on this boat! When did you have a chance to set all this stuff up in it?! It doesn't make any sense!"

"I did it last night. It was obvious you were plotting something to do with this lake."

"How'd you figure it out that *early...*?"

"Emai Lake is the most popular tourist attraction in the area. Yet, last night, when you were listing off the places you'd heard about when you 'went around town asking,' Emai Lake was *conspicuously absent* from your list of suggestions. What reason could you have had for not telling me about the most famous spot of all when I hesitated about whether to go? It was highly suspicious."

Now Lily understood why she had lost.

She had been too cautious for her own good. Once she knew she was going to use the lake to carry out her attack, she intentionally avoided mentioning it so he wouldn't figure it out. Her plan had been to invite him there while pretending she'd only just heard of it. However, that mistake had been her downfall.

She should have known.

Her opponent was a spy. Of course he'd know all the local attractions.

When she failed to mention Emai Lake, it was only natural that omission had caught his attention.

"Furthermore, Emai's shore would have too many tourists around. If you were going to make a play, it stood to reason it would be aboard a rental boat."

"But you couldn't have known I would pick *this* boat! I mean, it just happened to be the only one—"

"Exactly. It *just so happened* that there was only one boat left. You should have noticed how odd that was. And you should have wondered why, despite all the tourists clamoring to see the sunset over the lake, this boat and this boat alone remained unclaimed."

"Ah..."

"Look down by your feet—from the rower's point of view."

Lily, unsure what he meant, looked down at the boat.

Then she gasped.

It had been right under her seat all along.

A painted warning—OUT OF ORDER.

How had she missed it that whole time?

"It's a simple little trick," Klaus explained in a dispassionate tone.

"The thing is: Only the rower can see the warning. On that side, it's in your blind spot. But that was enough to prevent anyone else from using the boat. So because of how popular these rental boats are, it was natural that this would be the only one left."

When a man and a woman got in a rowboat together, it was easy to guess who would end up on which side.

The man would sit in the front of the boat to row, and the woman would sit across from him in the back.

When there was a warning only visible to the rower, the passenger would be unlikely to even notice it.

Her sole opportunity had been the moment she boarded, but back then, Klaus had diverted her attention by offering her his hand.

That was why Lily had overlooked his trap.

Klaus spoke again to seal the deal. "That concludes today's explanation. Lily—you aren't qualified to be my enemy."

Now realizing just how outclassed she was, Lily bit her lip in frustration.

"R-rgh... I can't believe you saw through my plan..."

To be honest, she was still having trouble coming to terms with that.

Klaus let out an exasperated sigh. "Furthermore, I actually knew you were planning to attack me from the moment you stepped into my room last night."

"Hwuh?! But how...?"

There was no way he should have been able to figure it out that fast!

Her eyes went wide with shock, and he gave her his answer.

"I just did."

"I feel stupid for even hoping to get a decent answer out of you!"

"Anyhow, hurry up and give me the antidote already. The boat's going to sink."

"I-I'm not happy about it, but you're right...," Lily replied as she reached into her pocket.

Immediately, she realized something was off.

"...Huh?"

"Hmm? What is it?"

"The antidote... It's not there..."

"Cut it out." Klaus sighed. "Trying to bargain at this point will just waste both our time."

He was telling her to accept her loss with grace.

"No, that's not what I'm doing... I really don't have it..."

"Again, I'm not going to fall for your—"

"I left it in my room by mistake..."

"...Excuse me?" Klaus's eyes went wide.

He looked even more shocked than he had when the blast of poison gas sprayed up in his face.

"...What kind of poisoner forgets her own antidote?"

"I was nervous! I'm terrible with this s-seduction stuff!"

"Seduction? Were you trying to seduce me?"

"Th-that's not important... So, um, Teeeeach? Any chance I can get you to unlock the shackle *without* the antidote?"

"No. My fingers are trembling too badly." Klaus looked down at his palm. "I'll have difficulty even swimming like this, much less lock picking."

"Ha-ha, I'll bet."

"........."

"........."

Klaus, still immobile from the paralytic, went silent.

Lily, unable to flee due to the shackle, went silent as well.

As they stared at each other, they heard a watery *ploosh* come from their feet.

The boat was starting to sink in earnest.

"...Lily, I have an order for you."

"...Yes sir."

"Row like your life depends on it." Klaus narrowed his eyes. "Because it does."

This was no bargaining technique.

Lily grabbed the oars—

"NOOOOOOOOO! I DON'T WANNA DIEEEEEEEEE!"

—and loudly screamed as she began rowing with all her might.

Despite his life being in just as much danger, however, Klaus was calm and collected.

"Don't worry. When I said it would sink in eight minutes, I was lying."

"Oh, thank goodness."

"It's actually nine minutes and five seconds."

"Okay, I'm still pretty worried!"

"Lily, just row like a cloud, and the oars will—"

"JUST SHUT UP AND HELP ME ROWWWWWW!"

Of course, the person who rendered him immobile was none other than hers truly.

As Lily made for the shore like a girl possessed, she lamented her blunders the whole way there.

The moment Lily reached the shore, she slumped in the boat and loudly exhaled. "We made iiiiiit."

The vessel was half inundated with water. They had only just barely escaped going under.

Instead of returning to the dock they set out from, their final destination was a piece of shoreline with no tourists around. The still-brilliant sunset, the lake illuminated by its radiance, and the birds flying after the sun made for a heartrendingly poignant scene that was theirs and theirs alone. Not that they had time to enjoy it, but still.

Having used up the last of her strength, Lily splayed out her arms and legs.

She'd survived. But now that the danger was over, all she had left was her current sad state of affairs.

"Ahhh, I blew it." She gazed up vacantly at the sunset. "I guess there's a reason we washouts wash out. I should've known I could never take on an elite spy."

"Don't be so hard on yourself. Your toxin worked well."

"Yeah, but you took it on purpose, right?"

"To test your strength, yes."

The poison must have worn off, as Klaus was already on his feet and playing with the local wildlife. Two little birds were perched atop his arm. His personality seemed to make him popular with animals, although the same definitely couldn't be said about humans.

Lily wanted to shout at him and say that if he had time to play with birds, he had time to unlock her ankle, but she wasn't in much of a position to make demands at the moment.

All she could do was moan.

"So I guess nothing's changed."

She hadn't solved a single one of her problems.

"I'm still a washout, you still can't teach, the Impossible Mission still has a ninety percent mortality rate, and the deadline's only gotten closer. I guess this is game over for me."

To top it all off, she had even committed the crime of poisoning a superior. There was no way she would get off scot-free for that.

Having failed in her attempt at coercion meant the only thing awaiting her was despair.

"All I ever wanted was to become a spy and help protect my country…"

Lily had struggled to the bitter end, never once giving up, and this is where it had gotten her.

She hadn't changed anything.

And she hadn't gained anything, either.

Her fate had been sealed long ago, and all she'd done by trying to fight it was make a fool of herself.

However, Klaus replied in a calm, gentle voice. "And I'm going to make that happen."

"Huh?" Lily sat up.

"Don't give up on that dream. Your foundations are solid. Our battle might have been little more than a game, but upon realizing the danger you were in, you were the first member of the group to act. For that, you get full marks. Magnificent."

"A-aw, you're gonna make me blush." Klaus dismissed the birds sitting on his arm and walked right up to Lily.

He then gave the leg shackle a light kick. For whatever inexplicable reason, the lock that had proven so obstinate popped right open.

"Lily, I'm appointing you Lamplight team leader."

"Hweh?"

"I'll still be the boss, but the girls need someone they can rally around. I don't know what you mean when you say you want to 'come into bloom,' but how do you feel about helping make this Impossible Mission a success as Lamplight's commander?"

Lily just stared at him, unable to make sense of what her ears were telling her.

Theirs was a team taking on the unheard-of task of specializing in Impossible Missions, and she had just been offered a key role.

To her, that was like manna from the heavens. A lone beam of light, shining down through the twilit darkness surrounding her.

She had left her spy academy determined to become something more than a laughingstock and a washout—and now a path was opening up before her that would allow her to do just that.

"I-if you really mean it, then...I'd be pretty darn happy to."

"Then it's official; you're the leader. Let's make this mission a success."

"O-oh, '*leader*'... That's got a nice ring to it..."

She began repeating the word to herself with a spellbound look on her face.

She thought she heard Klaus murmur "I see it doesn't take much to make her happy," but she quickly forgot he said anything.

"B-but wait, how? Aren't you still just as bad at teaching as you—?"

"No, I figured out a solution to that."

"You did?"

She cocked her head to the side, and Klaus gave her a nod.

"Thanks to you, I came up with an excellent way to teach you all."

When?

Lily wouldn't learn the answer to her question until the next day.

It was their fourth day at Heat Haze Palace.

All the Lamplight members were gathered in the main hall. The girls, expecting a lesson just as nonsensical as the last, wore gloomy expressions. Secretly, though, none of them had given up hope that the situation would miraculously turn itself around. They clung to the faint possibility that maybe the last lesson had all just been one big mistake— and that the real lessons were going to start at any moment.

As the group sat on the sofa, Klaus finally arrived.

He stood before them, his back ramrod straight.

Then, he crossed his arms, closed his eyes, and sank into silence. It looked like he was meditating.

Ten seconds passed.

Right when the girls started wondering what exactly their weirdo of a boss was up to, he finally spoke.

"Now, it's as you can see."

"What is?" the white-haired girl asked briskly.

"I was apologizing."

"The hell kind of apology was that?"

The girls' shoulders slumped. No miraculous turnaround was coming.

Seemingly oblivious to their dejection, Klaus coolly went on.

"I have a confession to make. To tell you the truth, I've never actually been a teacher or the boss of a spy team before."

"………"

"You're surprised, I take it?"

There was no point offering a comeback to such low-hanging fruit. The girls chose to let that one slide.

"Because of my inexperience, I worried you unnecessarily. I'm sorry for that. From here on, I intend to share all the information I'm able to. If you have questions you want answered, please don't hesitate to ask."

"All right, then I got two." The white-haired girl raised her hand, fearless as ever. She focused her fierce gaze on Klaus. "Who exactly are you?"

"I can't tell you that."

"Why'd you pick us?"

"I can't tell you that, either."

"Fuck off."

"As you're aware, there are restrictions on what information an operative can disclose. I would like to tell you those things, but there are very few confidential matters I can discuss openly. Even so, I recognize how important it is for us to develop mutual trust, as trust is core to a spy team. All I can do is convey my intentions, so I hope that will suffice for now."

Klaus took a deep breath and spoke.

"None of you are meant to be sacrificed. And I'm not going to let any of you die."

His eyes were as earnest as could be.

"Here's my promise to you: If so much as a single one of you dies, I intend to kill myself in atonement."

The girls gawked at him, their eyes bulging.

The strong will behind Klaus's words couldn't possibly be an act.

He wasn't lying.

He wasn't trying to trick them.

He well and truly intended to take on the Impossible Mission with them.

"B-b-but…," the brown-haired girl mumbled timidly. Her eyebrows slumped downward. "We're still washouts, so there's no way we can—"

Klaus tilted his head to the side. "I really don't get it."

"Huh?"

"Why do you describe yourselves as washouts?"

"W-well, that's…"

"I've been praising you this whole time, haven't I?"

How so?

Question marks popped up over the girls' heads.

"Just so you know, I was the one who handpicked this roster. I went to your academies and scouted you myself. You each have boundless potential just waiting to be unlocked. And how people are viewed can change greatly depending on what group they're in. You may have been washouts back at your schools, but here at Lamplight—you're all magnificent."

The girls let out a collective sigh of comprehension.

Lily could feel a kind of warmth spreading through her heart. That *was* what Klaus had been saying the whole time.

From the very first moment they met back in the foyer, he'd been calling his students magnificent.

When it came to his teammates, the man was a giant softy.

"Also, I've come up with a method to improve your skills." Klaus turned away from the girls and picked up a piece of chalk.

He then began using the blackboard for the first time and wrote large letters across it.

The message was succinct.

DEFEAT ME

As the other girls stared at the words in confusion, Lily was the first to catch on.

This was the teaching method that superhuman had come up with.

"Now, then." Klaus tossed his chalk to the side. "The rest of the day will be self-study."

Chapter 2

Coordination

It was their ninth day at Heat Haze Palace, and they were in a hallway on the second floor.

"A-are we really doing this...?"

The black-haired girl replied to Lily's feeble complaint with a graceful rebuttal.

"Of course. It's the only choice we have."

Even in a situation as tense as theirs, her beauty remained utterly unblemished. In fact, between her faintly flush face, the sweat dripping down her neck, and the sight of her holding her breath, her attractiveness bordered on risqué.

Suddenly, Lily got word from one of the other girls.

"This is the roof lookout. No problems here... The target's still bathing. I can't see much through the steam, but he hasn't gone anywhere..."

Lily relayed what she'd just been told.

The black-haired girl nodded, then gave the thumbs-up to their teammates standing by in the hallway.

"Are you ready, lights duty? Lock duty, do you have the combination lock ready to go?" After finishing the final checks, she brushed her hair back. "It's time."

Her gaze was focused forward—on the bathroom.

Heat Haze Palace had a large communal bath and a private bathroom, and the girls normally took their baths in the former. This time, though, they were headed somewhere different—the bathroom used by Heat Haze Palace's sole male resident.

Inside, they could hear the shower running.

"At 0700 sharp, we all go."

The black-haired girl laid out their plan one last time.

"Begin Operation: Attack Teach While He's Bathing!"

The spy team Lamplight had been reborn.

At the moment, its boss and his subordinates were engaging in a most peculiar form of training…

It all started five days ago, on Lily and the others' fourth day at Heat Haze Palace.

In the main hall, none of the Lamplight girls knew what to say.

In preparation for their so-called Impossible Mission, Klaus had given the girls a lecture—or rather, he'd tried to, but his dysfunctional teaching methods had left them at a standstill. He'd then called them together once more, only to scrawl *DEFEAT ME* across the blackboard before taking his leave. Baffling didn't even begin to describe it.

The sole member who vaguely understood what he was getting at was Lily, who had met with him the day prior.

She was also the first to notice the change on the blackboard's far end.

There were some new items under the Heat Haze Palace Communal Living Rules.

Rule ㉘: Anyone who makes the boss say "I surrender" will receive a reward.

Rule ㉙: The previous rule has no restrictions on time or method used.

Rule ㉚: Aim to stage at least one attack every twelve hours.

One of the girls let out a dumbfounded cry.

"What's up with *that*?"

The rest, still similarly unable to grasp the rules, blinked in rapid succession.

"I think it's a sort of new lesson..."

The demure speaker was a girl whose red hair was in a distinctive bob.

She had a tall, slender build and was eighteen years old. Between her lovely frame without an ounce of excess fat and her calm, mild voice, she seemed almost ephemeral. She gave off an impression like an exquisite piece of glasswork, in that she seemed liable to break if not handled with care.

She explained her theory in great detail.

"With this, our practice will bear a close resemblance to actual field-work. Negotiation, coercion, seduction... We'll have to create situations that allow us to manipulate our target. That's an essential skill for spies..."

At that point, it became clear to the others that she was probably the clearest-spoken of the group.

"I must say, though, '*no restrictions on time or method*'?" The black-haired girl elegantly tilted her head to the side. "No matter how strong Teach is, I daresay he doesn't stand a chance against us if we come at him seven on one. We could attack him while he's asleep; we could slip poison into his food; we could dig up dirt on him and use it as black-mail material... The task seems altogether too easy."

The redhead frowned. "I wouldn't be so sure."

"How do you mean?"

"Our opponent is an elite spy...which means he'll know all the stan-dard techniques inside and out..."

The black-haired girl licked her lips and smiled. "Well, well, well, now that's an interesting thought."

Most of the girls took Klaus's proposal as a challenge. Given their smiles, they seemed eager to rush off and attack him at any moment.

However, not everyone was on board just yet.

"Wait, hold up. Why're you all so excited about this?" the white-haired girl demanded in a commanding tone. "I get that the guy's strong, but remember how shit he is at teaching? You're seriously just gonna go do what he tells you? Me, I don't trust him one bit. He hasn't even explained what our actual goal is yet."

"Then this works out perfectly, does it not?" the black-haired girl replied.

"Huh?"

"Once we've attacked him, tied him up, and tortured him into surrendering, we can make whatever demands we want. We could interrogate him until he gives up those details, or we could even make him step down and have a new boss appointed."

"Oh, good point," her white-haired companion agreed.

The brown-haired girl turned to her with a fainthearted look in her eyes. "No, no, no. I have serious reservations about using a training exercise as an excuse to threaten someone..."

"If you've got problems with that, you're gonna have to take it up with Lily," the white-haired girl shot back.

"With Lily?"

"She already tried to coerce him. And her thing wasn't even for training."

"Isn't that just a crime?"

Lily scratched her cheek. "Hey, I only sprayed him with a *little* poison gas."

"Are you serious?" the brown-haired girl replied with a look of horror on her face.

By the end of the discussion, though, the team had collectively settled on carrying out an attack.

As it currently stood, they only had a vague sense of how powerful Klaus really was, and they naturally wanted to test how fit he was to be their boss. If they didn't think he was strong enough to take on an Impossible Mission, then the prudent thing to do would be to coerce him into disbanding Lamplight as Lily had.

The black-haired girl made a grand, rousing gesture as she summed up the group's thoughts.

"We're all in agreement, then. And this is a perfect opportunity. Teach is underestimating us. He thinks we're a bunch of washouts! So let's head on over and show him just what we're made of!" She raised her fist in the air. "Our goal will be to finish it within ten seconds!"

With a triumphant "Yeah!" her accomplices raised their fists in turn.

Sure enough, it took less than ten seconds for the dust to settle on their first attack.

The moment Klaus stepped out into the hallway, the girls rushed him with their training knives. They leaped at him from the ceiling, dashed toward him on the ground, surrounded him—and all found their legs tangled up in wire.

Their foreheads smacked against the ground as they toppled to the floor in unison.

"...That didn't even make for decent sport."

Klaus stepped on the trainees' backs as he continued down the hallway.

At that point, the voices questioning his new teaching method went silent.

As Lily reminisced on how they had gotten there, the corner of the black-haired girl's eyes began to twitch. The telltale signs of exhaustion were beginning to overwhelm her elegance.

"Hmm-hmm, you've made a fool of me for the last time. Never again..."

"You're really mad at him, huh?"

"When you make that many advances on a man and get spurned each time, you start to hold a bit of a grudge, yes."

In the five days since their new training had begun, the girls had suffered one ignoble defeat after another.

Klaus was like a brick wall.

Even once he'd gone to bed, if they crept so much as a single step into his room, they'd find him wide-awake. When they tried to lay traps in the hallway for him, he disabled them without breaking a sweat. When they gave up on subterfuge and came at him head-on, it always ended with them in cuffs. When they tailed him to find weaknesses to exploit, he invariably gave them the slip. And when the black-haired girl seductively asked him *"Say, Teach...want to have a good time in my bed tonight?"* he showed up at her room with a chess set, pummeled the girls lying in ambush there, then trounced them on the chessboard for good measure.

At first, they were just attacking him for educational purposes, but each time he bested them, Klaus would say—

"That didn't even make for decent sport."

—and their frustration grew that much harder to bear.

Now the emotion they felt for him was sliding dangerously toward outright animosity.

Let's make that pompous jerk eat his words!

Willing to put any and all options on the table, the girls ultimately decided to mount an assault on his bathroom.

Suddenly, Lily began to grow suspicious.

"Still, it seems awfully convenient. He's in the bath right when we wanted him to be."

The black-haired girl brushed back her lovely tresses. "Actually, I was carrying some coffee around earlier and 'accidentally' spilled it all over him."

"Whoa, good job actually hitting him."

"Mm-hmm, men are such simple creatures. Teach is probably at full mast in there with his head full of obscene fantasies about how he intends to punish me for my clumsiness. I bet he's picturing me in a maid uniform, baring my chest as I fawn over him and whimper *I'm so sorry, Master... How can I ever make up for this...?*"

"Uh...okay? I don't really follow, but your plan sounds a bit... mature." Lily blinked, only having understood about half of what she'd just heard.

"Don't believe everything she says, Lily. Sounds like her views on men are pretty damn twisted." The white-haired girl, who was on standby beside them, offered up a cool retort.

The black-haired girl cleared her throat. "If you have time to be saying things like that, then I take it you've done your job already?"

"Who do you think you're talking to? I snatched it ages ago—right out of his pocket." She proudly flashed them a key.

"Perfect." The black-haired girl chuckled. "Oh, I'm looking forward to this. He'll be right in the middle of his shower when all of a sudden the lights go out, the window gets blocked, and three members of the opposite sex come charging right at him. That should give him a good scare."

It sounded like she was enjoying it all a little too much.

"...Ten seconds until go time."

As she spoke, Lily and the other two members of the attack team closed their eyes and spent ten seconds acclimating themselves to the darkness. The moment they opened them back up, all the lights in the hallway and bathroom went out.

It was starting.

The three of them rushed into the bathroom as one.

Primed for the dark, they made it through the changing room with ease.

Then the white-haired girl reached the door to the bathroom proper. It was locked, but that was what the key she'd pilfered beforehand was for. She slid it into the lock.

"Huh?" Suddenly, her hands froze.

"Hurry it up!" the black-haired girl cried.

"It's not opening. Huh. Did he slip me a dummy or something?"

"*What?*"

"Welp, no choice. Time to smash the door in."

"So violent!"

The white-haired girl gave the door a mighty kick and sent it flying, lock and all. Choosing not to worry about how long it would take to fix later, the girls charged ahead.

All in all, the room was about a hundred square feet.

Inside, Lily spotted Klaus, who was standing up and holding a bar of soap. Luckily, it was too dark for her to get a decent view of his crotch.

She was a bit worried about the time they'd lost earlier, but Klaus's eyes still shouldn't have had time to adjust to the darkness yet.

All they had to do now was pin him down and tie him up. But just as Lily's heart began to soar—

"Woof!"

—Klaus let out a booming shout.

The man was normally so quiet, the room was pitch-black, and the bathroom walls were incredibly echoey.

The girls flinched unexpectedly.

Klaus took advantage of that opening to hurl his bar of soap, which flew with unerring accuracy and slid right beneath Lily's foot.

"I'm gonna"—Lily's body tilted at an inopportune angle—"faaaall!" She tumbled to the ground, taking the others down with her.

Once they fell, they realized that the floor had shampoo streaked all across it. Friction was a luxury denied to them.

The three attackers slid across the bathroom tile, only stopping when they slammed into the wall. They tried to stand, but due to the darkness, they couldn't see where the other two were and ended up tripping over one another's legs and collapsing back onto the floor.

"St-stay calm!" the black-haired girl cried. "The target doesn't have weapons. He doesn't even have clothes! We still have a chance!"

"Magnificent."

Klaus casually strolled over to the window. It was covered by the lid the girl on the roof had put over it, which Klaus smashed with the heel of his palm.

Sunlight streamed back in, clearing out the bathroom's darkness.

"The persistence you've displayed is admirable. However, your scheme was still sorely lacking."

Klaus stood up straight with the sunlight to his back.

He was still stark naked.

"Treat your target like a wild animal. Approach them as you would a buck galloping through a meadow, and observe them like you're admiring a squirrel making preparations to hibernate. You aren't ready to take on an Impossible Mission yet."

"...First things first—put on a towel," the white-haired girl demanded.

"Also, as you can see, a well-trained spy thinks nothing of being seen naked."

"Put on a towel."

"In turn, you all should be able to see me naked without a hint of emb—"

"Put on a towel."

Klaus wrapped a towel around his waist. He looked almost bored, but perhaps that was just their imagination. "...As I was saying, there's a lot of room for improvement, but all in all, it wasn't a bad attempt. Make sure there's another in the next twelve hours."

The black-haired girl chuckled elegantly and flashed him a smile.

"Oh, you think you can run? The bathroom door might be broken, but the changing room has a combination lock on it."

"I could just interrogate you three like usual"—Klaus strode past them and reached for the changing room door—"but luckily enough, I have a master key."

The lock popped open.

Wait—combination locks weren't even supposed to have master keys.

As the girls stared in him in shock, Klaus turned back around. "Right, and one other thing."

"Yeah?"

"Attacking me as part of your training is fine, but let's have this be the last time your impure motives spur you to attack me while I'm bathing."

"WHAT IMPURE MOTIVES?!"

They didn't know if he was serious or just joking, but either way, the humiliation they felt wasn't something they'd soon forget.

And so, the long string of defeats grew.

"Arrrrrrrrgh! Why can't we beat him?!"

"I saw Teach's you-know-what… The horror…"

"Hey, lemme give the orders next time. We can get him. I know we can."

"We should start by gathering intelligence. If we don't find some weakness of his…I don't think I like our odds…"

The girls were gathered around a table in the main hall, chattering among themselves and brainstorming about what kind of attack to launch and what they needed to improve. Their instructions were to attack once every twelve hours, so time was of the essence.

Klaus's new teaching style was already paying dividends. By repeatedly battling against an elite spy, the girls were rapidly amassing experience.

"There's one thing I don't understand, though. What exactly happened back there? The lock on the changing room shouldn't have opened like that."

The black-haired girl gracefully tilted her head to the side, prompting a "Hmm?" from one of her teammates. "You're not talking to me, are you?"

The speaker, a member of the team with messily tied-up silvery-cerulean hair, gave an insolent smile.

She was the kind of person it was difficult to get a read on. She was sixteen and had a medium build, but despite her reasonably good looks, she wasn't the type of beauty who turned heads. Even her hairstyle, the one distinctive thing about her, was hard to properly put a name to. All in all, the impression she gave off was "aloof."

"Don't act like this doesn't concern you. You were in charge of the lock, were you not?" the black-haired girl replied.

"Hey, I dunno what to tell you. I sealed the door with a combination lock, so unless he knew the six-digit code, it shouldn't have opened."

"...Look, just admit you made a mistake."

"Excuse me? Hey, if we're pointing fingers, the attack squad screwed up way worse."

"........."

The cerulean-haired girl was skilled, but those skills came paired with an unfortunate arrogant streak. Incidentally, she was the sole member of the group who had succeeded in opening her padlock within the time limit on the second day.

Lily clapped her hands together before the argument could get any more heated. "All right, all right, let's remember that the most important thing right now is teamwork—and the bonds we share. Let's all just take a deep breath. Here, you can each have one of the super-fancy financiers I bought."

"Oh my...this is sumptuous!" "Huh, that's good."

"Hee-hee, if you want another, all you have to do is bow down to your glorious leader!"

"Looks like *someone's* gotten a big head." One of her teammates good-naturedly heckled her, and the others joined in.

They were still a bit fuzzy on the details, but they had all come to accept Lily's new title.

They had their doubts about it, to be sure, but after hearing how ecstatic Lily sounded when she said things like—

"Whew, no matter how many times I say it, it always has such an nice ring. *Leader*... It's like the word itself is telling the world to watch out—golden girl Lily is on the stage, and this is where her legend begins. Hee-hee-hee..."

—they decided to let her have it.

After turning away from Lily, who looked like she was on top of the world, the others went back to brainstorming their plan of attack. No simple answer to their crisis seemed forthcoming, but their discussion was fervent all the same. Part of that was spurred by their resentment toward Klaus, but the bigger motivator was entirely rational.

One number was at the forefront of their minds—that 90 percent mortality rate.

Klaus had sworn he'd get them all back alive, but they couldn't afford to blindly trust that promise.

"In any case, it seems our only option is to work on our coordination," the black-haired girl concluded. "If we can't defeat a single man, then I find it hard to imagine us succeeding at the Impossible Mission."

"Hmph. Yeah, looks like that's all we can do for now."

The cerulean-haired girl scoffed arrogantly as she agreed. Then a thought occurred to her, and she looked over at her companion sitting on the couch a little ways from the table.

"Hey, you've been real quiet," she said before addressing her by name. "You got anything to add, Erna?"

The blond looked up with a vexed expression.

Her hair was dazzlingly yellow, and her skin was so fair, it was almost transparent. The frilly dress she was wearing only added to the image of a doll crafted by a master artisan. It wasn't just her appearance, either. Her taciturn nature accentuated the artificial ambiance around her. Out of all the Lamplight members, she was by far the least talkative.

At fourteen years old, she was also the group's youngest member.

She opened her mouth and reluctantly replied, "She's wrong."

Those were her first words of the meeting.

"What big sis Lily said. It's been bothering me."

"Hmm...?" Lily cocked her head to the side.

"All that talk about bonds is just pretty words. We're spies. We can't afford to trust one another so easily."

That was certainly a cold way of putting things.

The other girls all turned and stared at her. They couldn't understand why she would threaten to disrupt the team's unity given their situation. Their gazes held a mixture of reproach and confusion.

"Ummm, how about a nice financier?" Lily could tell all too keenly just how tense the mood was.

"I don't want it." Erna stood, paying no heed to Lily's blank expression. "...I'm going for a walk."

She had no intention of participating in the discussion.

Her rejection split the group into two camps: those who responded with anger and those who could say nothing at all.

However, Erna ignored both parties alike as she strode away.

Lily called after her. "Come on, Erna, you have to at least trust us. That's what being a team's all about."

Erna whirled around. "If you believe in anyone, you lose. That's what being a *spy* is all about."

Her gaze was as cold as ice.

A heavy silence descended on the main hall.

After leaving Heat Haze Palace, Erna walked through the twilit city.

With no particular destination in mind, she stood atop a bridge and watched a locomotive pass under it and bathe her in its steam. She then bought a crepe from a shop by the station and swayed side to side as she listened to the band performing in the main plaza. However, the church bells soon chimed six, and the noise startled her into dropping her crepe. She tried to take her mind off it by going over to a coin-operated music box, but when she put in her coin, it refused to start. After hitting it a few times, she gave up.

She really was just wandering.

Sometimes, the world could be divided into two groups of people.

For instance, there was the type who could leave an interaction with other people feeling satisfied with themselves versus the type who would invariably agonize over the things they'd done and said.

Erna was a prime example of the latter.

I went too far..., she thought, dejected and alone.

After leaving the station, she had aimlessly wandered down side roads.

All I wanted to do was remind them that spies need to remain vigilant and skeptical, so why did I have to say it like that...? I totally ruined the mood...

Streetlights were only installed in the larger roads, so the darkness on the side streets was especially thick. The sun hadn't totally descended past the horizon yet, but even its light was scarce.

Erna walked through the shadows with her shoulders slumped.

At this rate, they're going to abandon me during the mission...

She came off as aloof, but she was actually a very sensitive person. Yet, she also had a habit of exhibiting strange displays of pride, which only served to further isolate her from others.

For a spy, a bad relationship with one's teammates was an easy way to get killed.

Intellectually, she knew that, but...

Then I got so overwhelmed by my own awkwardness that I just ran away...

The stroll was just an excuse.

Truth was, she had fled in fear from the entire conversation.

I have to get back so I can apologize... Play up how cute I am and say Big sis Lily, I'm sorry... *But I can't get too close to them, or they'll get caught up in my situation...*

She knew what she needed to do, but due to her poor communication skills, her thoughts began straying.

"How unlucky..." Erna hung her head sadly.

And right when she did—

"Hey, kid. Hold up a second."

"Huh?"

—someone called out to her, and she stopped in her tracks.

When she looked up, she discovered two seedy-looking men covered in tattoos leering down at her. They strode toward her with wide gaits, cutting off all avenues of retreat.

Without noticing, she had wandered all the way over to the harbor, the area where the longshoremen lived. She had heard about how dangerous things were over there. The area was ripe with the stench of booze and raw garbage, and the brick buildings lining the street seemed liable to collapse at any minute.

A piece of information flitted back through her mind—that, around the harbor, there were men who'd gotten fed up with the backbreaking work on the docks and left to form groups that were decidedly less savory. The men before her were likely two such examples.

"Guessing from that nice outfit you're with the bourgeois. Say, you wanna step into an alley with us for a minute?"

"No… Get away from me…"

She tried to step back but discovered yet another man behind her. There were more than just two of them.

She shouldn't have been so careless.

She couldn't believe she'd let herself get surrounded.

"Hey, no need for this to get ugly. We're tryin' to help you out here. Let's all just be friends, what do you say?"

Friends?

Hearing that word, Erna replied in spite of herself. "I've got a question, mister… How are you supposed to make friends…?"

"Huh? You just make sure they know how strong you are." The man pulled a knife out of his pocket. "See, now you wanna be my friend, right?"

He pointed the knife straight at her. The threat of a weapon would usually be enough to ensure someone's cooperation.

"How unlucky…" Erna's nose twitched ever so slightly.

"Huh?"

"You said you wanted an alley… Is this one okay?"

Erna obediently began walking, and a vulgar smile spread across the man's face.

"See? Now you're bein' friendly, just like I said."

"………"

Crass as he was, the man had a point.

People were naturally drawn to the powerful. They wanted them as trusted allies. They wanted them as partners they could put their faith in.

If she wanted to get along with the others, all she had to do was show them her strength.

Having now realized that, she was struck by how obvious it was.

The answer was right before her, plain as day—she just needed to succeed where they had failed so many times.

"So, kid, who's your dad? Some sorta CEO? A politician? What say you introduce me to him sometime?"

"………"

"Don't go clamming up on me, now. Not unless you want me to cut that pretty little dress right off you."

The man approached her, interrupting her train of thought, and his companions moved to encircle her.

The alley was a dead end. There was nowhere to run.

"How unlucky…," Erna quietly said. "Gee, Erna, it's almost like that's how your entire life has gone."

She didn't mean to give them her name, but fortunately, the men didn't seem to notice. They looked at her, puzzled.

She kept talking. She needed to buy time until the moment struck.

Her nose twitched again.

"I always seemed to get myself involved in some kind of trouble. Day in, day out. Accidents, tragedies, disasters…"

"What are you mumbling about—?"

"But over time, I started to be able to tell. It was faint, but I could sense it. I could sense when and where the misfortune was coming."

It was time.

Erna could smell it.

"I'm code name Fool—and it's time to kill with everything."

She looked overhead.

The men followed her lead and peered up in turn. They shuddered.

It was raining bricks.

Dozens of them were falling from the sky.

While the men gasped in shock, Erna was already on the move.

The block they were on had many antique brick buildings, and chunks from their outer walls would sometimes crumble and fall due to decades of exposure to the elements. But unlike Erna, who had noticed the signs in advance, the men were frozen stock-still.

After hurrying out of the danger zone, she turned, looked at the men being buried in the rain of bricks—

"Good-bye, misters."

—and shot them a contemptuous look.

When Erna got back to Heat Haze Palace, Lily let out a shout.

"What happened to you?! You're filthy!"

In the few hours since they'd last seen each other, Erna had managed to cover herself entirely in mud. The hem of her skirt was also torn, leaving her fair thighs bare and exposed. She didn't seem injured, but she had clearly been through quite an ordeal.

In contrast to Lily's overt display of shock, though, Erna gave her a blunt reply. "This happens all the time."

"That's no way to explain—"

Before Lily could finish, Erna quietly cut her off. "I'll do the next attack."

"What…?"

"And I want you all to back me up with everything you have."

With that, Erna headed up the stairs.

All Lily could do was watch the lonely looking girl go.

"Is she really okay…?" she asked, more to herself than to anyone else.

Out of the blue, though—

"She really totally isn't!"

—a loud voice boomed right in front of her.

"Bwah!" Lily cried as she leaned back and looked down.

A short girl was standing before her.

Pleased that her prank had worked, she gave Lily an innocent smile.

Her hair's color could best be described as ash pink, and just like Erna, she was fourteen years old. She had a habit of shaking her long hair and swaying her short body side to side. No matter what was going on, she could always be found wearing the same cherubic smile, cute as an angel straight off a fresco.

"Erna and I went to the same academy for a while! So I know all the rumors, yo! They say she's really unlucky."

The pink-haired girl hopped up and down as she relayed the information, as if she was so excited to tell someone that she couldn't even contain herself.

"Unlucky?" Lily quietly replied. "That doesn't sound very scientific."

"It's true, yo! Someone I knew even got in an accident, and it was bad enough that they made Erna transfer!" Her glee as she recounted the awful story was disconcerting.

Maybe that was what had earned Erna the designation of problem child.

Lily knew all too well how easy it was for someone who couldn't work with their teammates to end up washing out.

"Wow, that's a really sad story…"

"It is?"

"W-wait, isn't that why you told me?"

"No, c'mon, listen to this!"

The pink-haired girl leaped up and whispered in Lily's ear.

"…Let's say Erna leads someone somewhere and something nasty happens to them. People will treat it like an accidental death instead of a homicide, yo! It's the ultimate assassination technique!"

Upon hearing this explanation, Lily's eyes went wide. She couldn't just laugh it off as unscientific anymore.

If someone could call forth misfortunate and distribute it to others… then that person could commit the perfect crime.

No weapon needed, no evidence to trace. They could take down their target and pass it all off as an accident.

Lily felt a chill run down her spine.

"If you need someone who specializes in accidents and disasters— then Erna's your girl!"

That fact wasn't just heartening, it was downright uncanny.

What exactly was she capable of if she used her powers to their fullest…?

One day, Klaus was out and about.

Thanks to the girls' recon efforts, they had a pretty decent handle on Klaus's daily routine. After waking up, he would go work up a sweat in the training room, then shower. After breakfast, he would spend the rest of the day reading through suspicious-looking documents and sending off telegrams to spy headquarters from his room. Once night fell, he would either head out or stay in his room and paint. When he did go out, it was probably to complete various solo missions, as his destination usually varied. As for meals, he cooked them all himself, preparing them in Heat Haze Palace's kitchen and then taking them back to his quarters to eat. Every few days, he would also go out to buy ingredients and various other sundries.

On one such day, Erna tailed him to an art store, then called out to him.

"Oh, Teach, what a coincidence…"

"I suppose it is." Klaus was holding a large, bulging paper bag. "Lily tripped over my paints last night and spilled them all, so I had to come buy more. Is it just you today?"

"It's my turn to go shopping. All the others are busy training for the next attack."

"Well, I'll be sure to look forward to it."

"I see…"

"……"

"……"

"……"

"……"

I need to keep up the conversation, or I won't be able to lure him in…

Erna wasn't great with words, and Klaus was taciturn by nature. Putting the two of them together wasn't exactly a winning recipe for a scintillating conversation.

For her plan to work, Erna needed to invite him to stroll around town with her.

No matter how hard she tried, though, she couldn't get the words *Want to come shopping with me?* out. The rest of her spy fundamentals were excellent, but her communication skills were sorely lacking.

If she didn't get herself to talk, the target would end up just heading home. But right as Erna began to panic—

"So what's on the shopping list?"

—Klaus spoke first.

"Huh?"

"What is it you're buying?"

The question did the trick, and Erna's tongue untied itself.

"G-groceries. And soap and an alarm clock. And my curtain got torn, so some fabric. And a new set of pajamas, if I find something cute."

"That sounds like a lot for one person to carry. Why don't I come along?"

She hadn't expected the target to throw her a lifeline.

However, she wasn't about to look a gift horse in the mouth. The two of them set off down a side street.

I'm sorry, Teach. This will only bring you misfortune.

She wasn't thrilled about having to use his kindness against him, but it was what it was. They lived in a world of subterfuge; by their own standards, what she was doing was downright tame.

Erna sniffed the air, and before long, she caught the scent she was looking for.

She had been diagnosed with what her old psychiatrist had called a predisposition for unluckiness.

Ever since childhood, her life had been plagued with misfortune. Despite being born to a family of wealthy aristocrats, she had lost both her parents in a tragic mansion fire. Trains she took would derail, and paths she walked down would be beset by hoodlums. She had even been grazed by lightning once or twice.

If anything could be said to be lucky about her, it was that she had survived this long at all.

After so many brushes with misfortune, she had gained an acute sense for bad luck.

It had a certain smell.

It was unclear how her olfactory power worked, but she could generally figure out when and where tragedy would strike.

I'll do what none of the others could and take down Teach. I'll trounce him. Then they'll all respect me, tell me how great I am, and gather around me; and this time, I'll be able to get along with them—and fulfill my dream.

As she casually guided her target, Erna chuckled to herself.

I'm code name Fool—and it's time to kill with everything.

It happened when they reached the main street.

The moment they got there, a shiny black vehicle came barreling toward them at full speed.

A runaway car.

Erna had smelled it coming, so she immediately leaped to the side. Even with fortune working against her, her spy training and preparedness allowed her to dodge it.

Just my luck..., Erna thought. *I knew something would happen, but I didn't realize it would be a runaway car. This is too much...*

She could sense the signs but never knew what would happen until it actually did.

The car charged onto the sidewalk, not slowing down in the slightest.

Klaus, seemingly unable to react to the imminent tragedy, didn't move an inch.

The other pedestrians screamed.

Erna fought back the urge to squeeze her eyes shut.

The car slammed into Klaus, and his body went flying through the air.

When it did, an odd popping noise rang out.

After hitting him, the runaway vehicle went into a spin, eventually coming to a stop just off the sidewalk. The tire tracks burned into the pavement made it terribly clear how violent the crash had been.

After soaring high into the air, Klaus's body tumbled limply back down—

"Well, that was close."

—yet his landing was a perfect ten.

What the heck?

Erna couldn't believe her eyes.

How could a man who'd just been run over be so completely unscathed?

He wasn't bleeding, had no visible wounds, and didn't seem the slightest bit shaken.

Klaus dusted himself off, then walked over to her.

"Are you hurt?"

"T-Teach…no injuries?"

"I can't say for sure, but nothing major, I think. I wouldn't mind giving him a piece of my mind, but I'd best let the police handle that. We've drawn enough attention as it is."

"Not the driver! You!"

"It's as you can see."

Klaus set off as calm as could be, as though to say that she was the odd one for even asking. Not only was he uninjured, his clothes weren't even soiled.

He must have leaped off the car's hood the moment it made contact—a feat requiring such precise timing that if he'd been a second early or late, it could have easily proven fatal.

Erna looked over at the motionless car.

What exactly had made it spin like that?

What exactly had been that popping noise?

"I punctured its tire." Apparently sensing her confusion, Klaus explained what had happened. "If nobody stopped that car, someone might have died."

"You did that in that tiny time...?"

"Would you like to know how?"

"No, that's okay."

"All you have to do is stab the tire with a knife."

"...I expected as much."

As they shared their silly little exchange, Erna pulled herself together.

The man beside her was a monster who operated in a different realm than normal people. Even getting hit by a car didn't so much as slow him down.

B-but...the unlucky smell is still there...!

This was no time to start feeling guilty.

After all, there was a real danger that standard misfortune wouldn't be enough to even put a dent in him...

Unfortunately, Erna's prediction was right on the mark.

No matter where she led him, Klaus evaded her bad luck with ease.

At one point, they headed down a side street only to have a pot full to the brim with boiling water fall off a food truck and topple right toward them. It took everything Erna had to get out of the way, but Klaus didn't even try to dodge. Instead, he caught the pot right out of the air and covered it with his leather coat.

He didn't let so much as a single drop spill.

Then, in a residential area, they ran into a vicious hound.

Erna didn't know what she had done to offend it, but the moment their eyes met, it bared its vicious-looking teeth and charged right at them. Its chain loose, the mad dog leaped at her so fast, no human could possibly get away, and yet—

"What a lively pup."

—a light palm strike on the jaw from Klaus was all it took to settle the dog.

Meanwhile, Erna hadn't tried to flee. Her knees simply rattled.

From there, they headed into an alleyway, and just like with the thugs the day before, a rain of bricks came toppling down on them.

When they did—

"Ah, crap," Klaus said with some embarrassment. "A few of them cracked."

—that embarrassment was prompted by something utterly trivial.

The extent of his failure had been that in catching the fourteen bricks out of the air, he had been unable to preserve them all in perfect condition. He'd even had time to comfort the young woman cowering nearby.

He really is a monster...

She scowled at him, but Klaus's expression was as cool as always.

The more time passed, the more depressed Erna got.

Not only was her target doing as well as ever, it wasn't even clear if he realized he was being subjected to ill fortune at all. He was the definition of cool and composed as he continued helping her shop. The bags of groceries should have weighed him down, but he had yet to voice a single complaint about Erna's instructions.

Meanwhile, Erna was being reminded of something all over again.

Specifically, just how fearsome her power was.

I really am a dreadful child...

Normally, she would never follow the scent of misfortune so many times in a row. Usually, she headed straight in the opposite direction.

If he was anyone else, he probably would have gotten hurt really bad over and over...

Each time she brushed shoulders with misfortune, she always imagined a voice whispering in her ear.

This tragedy happened because of you, it would say.

The only reason things had turned out okay was because the person she was with defied all norms. But what if it had been a young girl, like her? What if it had been one of the other Lamplight members? Would they still be willing to be friends afterward? In fact, wouldn't the man by her side want to leave her, too, if he found out about her power?

I should just give up on making friends with people…

Who was it who had first spread those rumors at her spy academy? she wondered.

"You'd be better off staying away from that girl."

And how long would it be before the same thing happened at—?

"That's everything you needed, right?"

As Erna sank into the mire of her own thoughts, she suddenly heard Klaus's voice.

She came to her senses with a start.

They had successfully acquired all the items she'd listed off back at the start. They had just left the last store, and Klaus was cradling a box of detergent under his arm.

All that, and her target didn't seem the slightest bit fatigued.

"Y-yeah, it is. But there's still a few places I want to—"

"I think this farce has run its course."

Klaus stopped in place.

When Erna turned her head to look at him, she found him staring down at her in turn with a calm gaze. A chill ran down her spine, and she began sweating all over.

Wha…?

He was calm but terrifying.

He opened his fingers, and the paper bag he was holding fell to the ground. He didn't seem to be in any rush to pick it back up.

"To tell you the truth, the teachers at your academy told me about your ability. They called you the girl who attracts misfortune."

"……!"

"Now I finally understand the truth behind that warning."

He had known all along.

Everything he'd done had been an act. All of Erna's attacks had been exposed from the start. He'd probably just accompanied her to test her powers.

Klaus turned toward Erna and reached for her.

The moment he did, she immediately remembered all the times he had hurled the Lamplight girls through the air.

Her eyes snapped shut.

There was no escape…

"People really misunderstand you, don't they?"

However, it was the exact opposite of what she'd feared.

He gently rubbed her head.

"If anything, the unluckiest thing of all was that a girl with your talents never got properly praised for them."

"Huh? Whaaaauh?" she yelped, unable to understand what was happening.

"You did good." Klaus nodded affectionately. "And the way I see it? You're the luckiest girl in the world."

Erna could hardly comprehend what he was saying.

Beneath his hand's warm weight, her former psychiatrist's words flashed through her mind.

"All right, miss. Here's the diagnosis.

"You have a predisposition for unluckiness…or at least, that what I'm calling it for the sake of convenience. Now, no condition that unscientific actually exists.

"Perhaps it would be more accurate to call it a desire for punishment.

"I remember reading about that mansion fire…and about the young girl who was its sole survivor.

"Because of that incident, you've become obsessed with the notion that your own survival is unfair. It causes you to subconsciously pursue punishment.

"The closest analogy would probably be to how suicidal individuals sometimes cut their wrists. Much like how such people make failed suicide attempts, you seek punishment—but not of the capital variety. At the end of the day, it's a mechanism you use to regulate your emotions. That's what drives you to seek punishment but not death.

"Because you survived, your dream is to save as many people as you can… Objectively speaking, that's pretty darn intropunitive.

"You need to stop blaming yourself. When you do, it drives you to seek punishment all over again.

"Or at least, you need to try...though breaking that cycle will be easier said than done."

As far as rational explanations for Erna's powers went, that one probably hit the mark.

Erna was drawn to misfortune because she unknowingly sought it out. Though her conscious mind could suppress the urge, her unconscious mind was continuously finding circumstances to punish herself and was driving Erna toward them.

They told her not to blame herself, but how could she possibly not?

It would be one thing if the only person who got hurt was her, but her misfortune often dragged everyone around her into it as well—even people she cared about. People who were kind to her.

For ages, she had seen herself as wretched, disgusting, shameful.

Of course, she hadn't made a single friend back at the academy.

So why was the man before her kindly praising someone so terrible...?

"Countless people were saved thanks to you. That runaway car could have crashed into some of the other pedestrians. That pot could have easily toppled over and splashed the people walking down that street. The mad dog could have bitten a child, and those bricks could have fallen on that woman."

"Huh?" Erna let out a flustered cry.

He certainly had a point.

All the misfortunes she'd experienced that day had happened in places with other people around. If Klaus hadn't been there to deal with them, they would have claimed other victims.

Guided by Erna's hand, Klaus had saved them all.

Now that he mentioned it, there was some truth to that, but...

"Th-that was an accident, though!" Erna's voice grew louder. "That wasn't the point! I was guiding you around to try to hurt you! The plan was to wear you down and have everyone come and attack you. Helping those people was just a coincidence!"

Now she was giving up their entire plan. Even she didn't know what had gotten her so agitated.

"I'm bad luck! An ill omen! People hate me! You can't call me lucky—it just pisses me off! You don't know what you're talking about. And don't go patting my head like a child, either! The person you're talking to is a monster—a demon who drowns people in misfortune for her own twisted satisfaction!"

"Well, I haven't been drowned in misfortune."

"Th-that's..."

"Don't move; you have some dust in your hair."

Still marching to the beat of his own drum, Klaus reached over and stroked Erna's head again.

Why isn't he scared to touch me...?

Panicking, Erna shook his hand off.

Why is he still looking out for me after I put him through so much?! How can he be so calm when he knows about my power and how I used it against him?! How could anyone possibly be so—?

"What's wrong, Erna?" Klaus asked. "...Are you crying?"

".........I."

"Hmm?"

"I!"

"You?"

"I-I'm not...crying...!"

"I see." Klaus chose not to point out how obvious her lie was.

Erna couldn't help but feel touched by his kindness. She even felt warm inside despite her efforts to resist.

"At any rate, your luck proved a great boon to the citizens of our nation today. I think that merits a reward. Is there anywhere you'd like me to take you?"

Erna shook her head. "How should I know something like that?"

"I promise it's not a trick question."

"It's just...it's the first time." Erna wiped at the corners of her eyes. "The first time in my life anyone's asked me on a date."

"...I see. In that case, I supposed I'd best take the lead."

Offering no resistance to the term *date*, Klaus slowly resumed walking.

By that point, Erna had completely forgotten she was supposed to be attacking him.

Klaus had assured her that the cheesecake was unrivaled across the entire Din Republic, and its flavor was just as exquisite as promised. The fact that the restaurant was both underground and members only had put Erna on edge, but the moment she bit into her dessert, all her fears melted away. Its texture was so smooth, it practically melted in her mouth. Despite being raised in an upper-class family, it put every other dessert she'd tasted in her life to shame. She cleaned her plate in the blink of an eye.

Klaus polished his slice off as well, then ordered seconds for both of them.

"My mentor took me here, back when I was a child. As a reward."

It was rare for him to ever talk about his past. Apparently, even the mysterious man before her had once had a teacher himself.

Strangely pleased by the thought, Erna replied with a story of her own.

"You wouldn't believe how rough I've had it! When I was first coming to Heat Haze Palace, my train got into an accident, and then the bus I was supposed to get on skipped my stop, and when another one finally came, its tires blew out!"

"I see your tongue's loosened up a bit."

"W-well, it's embarrassing when you point it out…"

"No, I understand the feeling. When I'm around people I trust—around my family—I become a far bit more eloquent myself."

"It's the same for me!"

As their conversation went on, Erna suddenly felt a sharp sting in her nose.

It was the smell of misfortune. And it was fairly intense, too.

Klaus, eagle-eyed as ever, noticed her discomfort. "What's wrong?"

"I-it's nothing…" Erna hesitated.

If I tell him, he might leave…

She couldn't predict misfortune down to its exact particulars.

All she could do was guess based on its smell. After all, that ability to sense a small portion of some bad luck that might befall her wasn't sufficient to tell her any specifics.

However, the scent she smelled now was acrid enough that she would normally have stayed away from it at all costs.

But...Teach will be able to handle it, right...?

She wanted to test him. She wanted to see if this man would stay by her side, no matter what.

It was an arrogant, childish way of thinking, and she knew that fact full well.

However, her desire to find out if Klaus was someone she could believe in won out.

In the end, he might end up leaving her, too.

But if he didn't, she wanted to see it with her own eyes.

Erna boldly leaned forward.

"Teach, I want you to come with me."

Their destination was a deserted alleyway sitting by a row of harbor warehouses.

It was late enough that the market had long since closed, and the streets were empty and still. They could hear the sound of waves lapping against the wharf. The sea off the harbor was a dark indigo even in the middle of the day, and at night, its hue seemed all the more ominous. Countless shipping containers waiting to be loaded into the warehouses were piled high, casting shadows like those of a humongous castle.

Erna clamped both hands over her nose.

The area was blanketed in an aroma so thick it was almost choking. It was the scent of misfortune that only she could sense, burning into her nasal cavity.

Her heart felt like it was going to burst out of her chest.

Normally, she didn't plunge herself into harm's way like this unless it was absolutely necessary.

She couldn't even begin to imagine what awaited them.

As she held her breath, Klaus came to an abrupt stop.

"Erna, I take it you've noticed," he said. "But we're surrounded."

She hadn't.

Suddenly, men came pouring out from behind the warehouses, one after another. There were eight assailants, and they moved to surround Klaus and Erna with guns in hand. Given their menacing expressions, it was fair to assume that they were on the wrong side of the law.

Klaus frowned. "Who are you?"

One of them, a man with a facial tattoo, barked out a threat. "Don't move. We've got a hostage."

"Excuse me?"

"We know who you are. Councilman's daughter and her bodyguard, right?"

Klaus cocked his head to the side. "Who? I'm afraid you have us mistaken for someone else."

"Heh, I figured you'd say that. But see, we did our research."

The men surrounding them were grinning mockingly.

"Councilman's daughter's not gonna run away and leave a constituent to die, is she? And it's no use playin' dumb. We know all about who you two are."

Evidently the "constituent" referred to the hostage they'd taken.

Erna couldn't make any sense of what was happening. "What's going on?" she whispered to Klaus.

"I don't know. It seems they're laboring under a misunderstanding, but...I think we can assume they're not interested in listening to reason."

The men appeared to be confident in their information.

Erna huddled next to Klaus. "...Teach, are you going to take them down?"

"........"

"Teach?"

Klaus let out a sigh. "No point."

"Huh?"

"They're telling the truth about the hostage. We have no choice but to do as they say." Klaus's voice was as cold as ice.

Erna lost all hope. This was beyond her expectations. This misfortune was too great.

She had no ability to deal with it herself, and Klaus raised his hands in a show of nonresistance.

"Get the chains," the tattooed man spat. "Tie 'em up, then stick a lock on and seal the keyhole with wax. Make sure not even an elephant could get out."

Klaus let out a faint sigh—a fact that didn't escape Erna's ears.

The chains the men used were almost half an inch thick. Trying to break them would be a fool's errand. And the padlock fastened to them was coated in wax, so trying to pick it wasn't an option, either.

Even if just by coincidence, the men had come up with the perfect countermeasure against Klaus.

How unlucky, Erna moaned to the heavens.

Erna and Klaus had their bags taken from them and were then forced into a car. After riding for two hours, they finally arrived at a cabin on the edge of town. That must have been the ruffians' hide-out. They could scream all they liked, but nobody would be able to hear them.

Erna kept a watchful eye on the ever-dependable Klaus, but he showed no signs of trying to resist.

"Wait here until the boss shows up."

The thugs shoved them into the cabin's shed, then locked it from the outside.

The shed was so small that just the two of them sitting was enough to make it feel cramped. It was also damp, not to mention dark due to the lack of proper windows.

Beside her, Klaus wriggled and squirmed.

That earned him a sharp "Move any more, and I'll shoot!" from their guard.

The man glared at them through the shed's one small slit.

"Opening the lock was a nonstarter," Klaus whispered. "We can't move, there are no windows large enough to escape through, and there's an armed guard. I assume they're communists who fancy themselves revolutionaries, but they shouldn't be this competent. Just who are these people?"

He must have already tried picking the lock—and failed.

"What about the other girls? The plan was to wear me down and have them attack me, wasn't it?" Erna softly shook her head. "They took my transmitter. I don't have a way to send them our location."

"Well, that's unfortunate."

"I'm sorry, Teach," she finally said. "This is my fault... This is all because I led you there..."

"It isn't. The only ones to blame are those men."

"I always bring bad luck to people. I get them wrapped up in things and hurt them... That's why I always wanted to save loads of people someday. But I could never work with others..."

"......"

"I guess it'd be better if I just stayed away from people..."

Klaus had been dragged into this because of her. A test for the sake of her own shallow insecurity.

Erna bit down on her lip.

In that moment, she would have been willing to take any punishment necessary if it meant Klaus's life would be spared.

"........."

Klaus remained silent.

She peered at him from the side, but his face was so expressionless, she had no idea what was on his mind. "You're really too hard on yourself. Looks like I'd best get us out of here."

"...You have a plan?"

"Something like that. But there are still a lot of things we don't know about our foes." Klaus sucked in a deep breath. "Time to break out the master key." With a lighthearted murmur ("After all, it's not like they pose us any real threat"), he got to work.

A little while later, someone opened the shed door.

From there, they were taken to the cabin proper. Ten sketchy-looking men were waiting for them in its living room. One of them, ostensibly their boss, was sitting in the group's center and being attended by the others.

"Hey there, kid. Remember me?"

Erna recognized his face. "From yesterday..."

It was the man who'd approached her in the alley the day prior. He was covered in bandages, but although he'd suffered serious injuries, it would seem they hadn't been fatal.

How unlucky...

Erna had assumed he was just a small-time thug. She never imagined he was the leader of a group ten-people strong.

"So I hear your dad's a councilman, huh? See, I just wanted to run you over, but then I found out I'd be better off abductin' you instead of killin' you. So change of plans."

"You mean that runaway car was—?"

"Yeah, I'm the one who put a hit on that cheeky little ass of yours. But hey, don't worry. Once I heard the good news, I decided to kidnap you instead. Your ransom money'll be put to good use in our revolution."

His injuries looked painful, and he winced as he stood up. Despite his claim that he no longer planned on killing her, his eyes burned with a hunger for vengeance.

Erna's knees went weak.

When the man stepped forward and reached toward her, Klaus spoke. "Don't touch her."

Despite having his entire body bound in chains, Klaus's tone was the same as ever. The man was unshakable. He continued without a shred of trepidation in his voice.

"This isn't necessary. Set us free this moment, and I'm prepared to overlook all this."

He let out an exasperated sigh.

"Your group is so minor, the police aren't even keeping tabs on you, right? You aren't worth my time."

That dismissiveness only stoked the man's rage.

"You think you're so tough, huh?!" he roared, then socked Klaus in the face.

Klaus groaned and collapsed to the ground. To Erna, it had looked like he'd turned his head to absorb the blow, but she couldn't be certain one way or the other.

"I know all about you, too. Some hotshot bodyguard, right? But with those chains and that keyhole blocked, you're just a big ol' punching bag."

The man gave Klaus a sharp kick.

"I almost feel bad for ya, but you brought this shit on yourself. Bet you've been livin' pretty good as the kid's bodyguard, huh? Filthy bourgeois lapdog!"

As the man finished his speech, he kicked Klaus right in the face.

A moan of pain escaped Klaus's lips, and it sounded genuine.

The ringleader stomped on Klaus over and over, and the spy gritted his teeth each time.

"You just sit there and stay quiet. You gimme any more lip, and it'll be the last thing you do."

The man had worn himself down and was breathing heavily. After giving Klaus one last kick, he turned back toward Erna.

Now it was her turn.

Tears began welling up in the corners of her eyes.

The moment he approached her, though, a determined voice rang through the room once more.

"You get one more warning." Klaus, visibly pained, rose to his feet. "Don't you touch her—you filth."

The ringleader returned his attention to Klaus. "You have any idea what sorta position you're in, bud?" His tone was thick with annoyance. "Change of plans. They said not to kill you 'cause you'd make for a good bargaining chip, but eh, fuck 'em."

"…Amusing—but false. Where exactly did you get that information?"

"None of your business!"

As the man shouted, he drew his gun.

His underlings immediately shouted "Boss!" to try to stop him.

However, their leader was undeterred. He leveled his gun straight at Klaus.

Even staring down its muzzle, though, Klaus's composure never broke. "Was it, by any chance…a young girl?"

"……" For a brief moment, the man looked shaken, but then he placed his finger on the trigger. "Just die!"

"Teach!" Erna screamed.

A gunshot echoed through the air.

Klaus's body twitched ever so slightly.

The men around them reeled back.

"Magnificent."

Klaus had used the chains wrapped around his body to block the bullet.

Still bound, he rose to his feet.

Their captors froze, their mouths agape. None of them had realized Klaus possessed such talents.

"Oh, this is getting to me. I don't even remember how long it's been since the last time I felt this elated." Yet, despite his words, Klaus's expression was as level as always.

"It was too well orchestrated to be a mere coincidence. You had us mistaken for someone else, yet the countermeasures you used against me were all but flawless."

The group's boss fired off a second shot, then a third. It was like he was trying to erase the sight before him.

Klaus blocked them all with his chains.

Eventually, when his foe exhausted the last of his bullets, Klaus continued speaking.

"Let me guess. After failing to run the girl over, you ran into another girl with...silver hair, I'd imagine. Then, under the pretense of idle gossip, she fed you a number of lies about us. Believing them, you decided to kidnap us. As for the hostage, I imagine you picked a dark-haired girl you just happened to run into? And it was a white-haired girl who told you where we were headed. Am I on the right track?"

"How could you possibly...?"

The boss's eyes went wide. Klaus must have been right on the money.

Klaus exhaled. "I must say, I'm impressed. In just ten short days, they've come farther than I could have possibly dreamed." Then, his voice grew quiet. Low enough to be more of a whisper only Erna could hear. "Goodness, though. They really went this far? Just for a lesson—just to *catch me*—you manipulated an *entire criminal posse*? It's no wonder I didn't notice. Those men took their hostage in earnest, and when they threatened us, they meant every word. Brilliantly played."

He then returned to his normal volume.

"Those girls are filled with boundless potential. I knew I chose well."

Unable to hold it in any longer, the ringleader let out a furious bellow.

"Quit your mumbling! You're a dead man!" Since shooting Klaus hadn't worked, the man drew a knife.

"There's just one thing I want to know." Klaus gazed at his captor in abject boredom. "How much longer should I keep playing along with this game?"

With this question, all hell broke loose.

Every one of the cabin's windows shattered simultaneously.

The criminals cried out in shock at the intruders—who just so happened to be the rest of Lamplight's members.

With an arrogant smirk, the cerulean-haired girl smashed her fists into the lackeys' jaws, one after another, and Lily followed up by stabbing them with poisoned needles and putting them to sleep.

Meanwhile, the redhead deftly wove her way through the mayhem and made for Erna and Klaus.

"I'm sorry, Erna…" Her voice was calm and quiet. As she spoke, she withdrew a large pair of shears and cut through Erna's chains *and Erna's alone.* "You gave us more luck than we bargained for, so after the first accident, we had to quickly amend the plan…"

Lily and the cerulean-haired girl added their own comments.

"Hey, I was against it, for the record!" Lily said. "I told the others I didn't want to put you through all that!"

"Trying to cover your own ass, huh?" the cerulean-haired girl shot back.

Klaus looked down in apparent exasperation. "First things first—deal with the men. I expect you to take less than two minutes."

With those words to motivate them, the young spies swept through the room at a record pace.

The cerulean-haired girl used her overwhelming speed to mow down foe after foe, and Lily used her sleeping poison to keep them down. It sounded like the other girls were outside, as a number of gunshots and men's screams rang out, but both noises soon died down.

Erna simply stared as she watched her teammates work.

"I see I've assembled quite the formidable team." Beside her, Klaus shrugged. "Erna, these are people you can work with."

"Huh?"

"Lamplight is the same as me—the kind of misfortune you bring isn't enough to kill us by half."

By the time the designated two minutes were up, all the criminals were unconscious and bound.

The pink-haired girl held up a large bag. "Yo, I found illegal drugs down in the basement!" That would give the police more than enough to arrest the whole gang once they handed them over.

There was just one more thing that needed settling.

The girls moved to surround Klaus's chained body.

At their center, Lily puffed up her chest with pride.

"Give it up, Teach! We got you this time!"

"I never imagined you'd go to such extremes. I could have been killed."

"It'd take more than a couple bullets to kill you, wouldn't it?"

The full scope of their plan was now clear.

When Erna almost got run over, the girls had realized the criminal group was after Erna's life, leading them to revise their initial plan. Their new scheme was to let the brigands bind Klaus, then swoop in afterward and take them out.

The plan had come dangerously close to crossing a moral line but had ultimately brought them success.

Their target, Klaus, was trussed up in thick chains and unable to move.

"All right, Teach. The cops'll be here in the next five minutes."

"You already made the call? Clever."

"Tee-hee. Y'know, Teach, you're gonna end up getting arrested, too, at this rate. And I gotta say, it's pretty lame for a spy to end up getting interrogated by his own country's police. Of course, I could be convinced to let you go if you surrender, then lick my boots while calling me Lily the Gr—"

"Now, then."

Suddenly, they heard a cracking sound, like a cookie being snapped in half.

"Huh?" the girls all said in unison.

Klaus gave his body a light shake, and his chains toppled to the ground. Just like that, he was free.

Lily delicately picked up one of the broken chains. Despite being half an inch thick, it had been ripped clear through.

"B-but these chains... They were designed for tying up wild game..."

"Next time, bring ones built for stopping dinosaurs." Klaus cracked his joints, then turned his gaze to the girls. "You lot aren't qualified to be my enemies."

Erna closed her eyes. She didn't need to look to know what would happen next.

All that reached her were the sounds.

From what she could tell, the rest of the team didn't last twenty seconds before getting launched through the air.

◇◇◇

It was well into the night, and they were all back in Heat Haze Palace's main hall.

"How the hell did we go to such lengths and still not beat him?!"

"This is starting to bum me out, yo! Feels like all our plans end with us getting blasted one way or another!"

"I guess that's our boss for you... We might even have to drag the police into it next time..."

The girls were deep into their now-regular post-mortem meeting. Tables were being slammed, and arguments were being had.

The plot they'd concocted this time around had been so ambitious, it had startled even Klaus, leaving them all but certain of their victory. They had even succeeded in capturing him. However, that victory had crumbled before their very eyes, and that fact made their discussion more heated than ever.

"We'll need to reconsider our strategy from the ground up," the black-haired girl gracefully declared. "Capturing our target doesn't seem possible, and our attacks are useless. We need to find some secret or vulnerability of his and exploit it to coerce him."

"Didn't we already rule that option out?" The cerulean-haired girl shot her an arrogant scoff. "And we all know how your attempts at seduction went."

"Rgh! That first time was just a fluke! There isn't a man alive who can resist my—"

"Sounds like someone's hankering for another late-night chess session."

"The man defies all logic! A girl comes to his room late at night and says *I can't sleep*, and he asks if she wants to play chess. She says *Let's do something* really *fun*, so he takes out his chess set. And when she whispers *Be gentle with me*, he offers her *piece odds*! Who *does* that?!"

"Maybe he just really likes chess."

"Fine, then how about we hear your big idea? As you may recall, we're dealing with a man who broke through a combination lock and ripped through chains designed for big game hunting. How exactly do you intend to capture a—?"

"All right, all right, break it up!"

As the discussion threatened to get ugly again, Lily loudly clapped her hands. Before the other girls had a chance to say anything more, she stuffed their mouths with baked goods.

"Remember, the most important things right now are teamwork and the bonds we share. Here, have another deluxe financier."

"So good…" "It really is sumptuous…"

"Heh. A leader's work is never done."

Having successfully cooled down the heated debate, Lily let out a pompous sigh.

Beside her, the redhead spoke softly.

"Hmm… At the moment, capturing him still looks to be our best option."

"You're not wrong, but…"

"It's really worrying. If we can't even capture a single man, then I don't like our chances on the Impossible Mission."

Hearing the situation in such unambiguous terms cast a heavy pall over the room.

Nobody had any rebuttals to that. Lily tried to cheer up the group, but without anything concrete to work with, her encouragement did little to lighten the mood.

Then—

"U-um…" Erna's face went red as she raised her hand. "Wh-when he broke the chains, there was a trick to it!"

The words came out a good deal louder than she'd intended. Her lips quivered, and when she spoke next, her face was even redder than before. "…When we were captured, Teach spit out a jewel he'd kept hidden in his mouth and used it to bribe the guard into damaging the chains with his gun."

"Oh!" the black-haired girl replied. "Now that you mention it, he said something similar back in the bathroom. About a squirrel making preparations to hibernate…"

Put more plainly, what Klaus had been trying to tell them was that many spies kept weapons and valuables hidden inside their bodies.

Klaus had used the jewel combined with his oratory skills to buy off the guard. Then, he intentionally provoked the ringleader into shooting him and further damaging the already-weakened chains. Even chains of that thickness would shatter after so many bullets.

Of course, Klaus had made sure to retrieve his gem on the way out.

"Jewels and riches—bribery. That's the master key that can open any lock."

"So that's what he used…," the cerulean-haired girl murmured.

Erna went on and offered her theory. "I think he opened our combination lock the same way. He must have bribed one of us ahead of time and had whoever it was tell him the password."

"Y-you mean one of us is a spy?!" Lily cried. She recoiled and cast dubious gazes at the other Lamplight members.

"We're all spies," the white-haired girl pointed out coolly.

After that, though, the girls went quiet.

They had a new problem to deal with—and a pressing one to boot.

"Now that I think about it," the black-haired girl said, "there was one person who always made sure to avoid letting fingers get pointed when we talked about the lock."

"Yeah!" the pink-haired girl added in her innocent tone. "Someone who was always going on about *trusting one another* and *the bonds we share*, yo!"

Their cerulean-haired teammate agreed with that line of reasoning. A smug grin spread across her face.

"Hey, Lily. Got a question for you."

"Hweh?"

"Where exactly did you say you got those financiers, again?"

Lily froze.

Sweat dripping down her brow, she let out a faint "Remember, the most important thing is the bonds we share…"

«««««««««   »»»»»»»»»»
. . . .

None of the others were interested in her platitudes.

Lily shrank backward to distance herself from her teammates, but she soon came up against a wall. Her lips quivered.

"I—I was just…uh, you know. Teach made it sound like such a good idea! He said it'd help me practice lying and help you all practice doubting your allies. And wow, we really learned a lot! After all, having one of your teammates double-cross you is the kind of thing that can totally happen out in the field! Good going, Teach! And good on me for going along with it! Sometimes a leader has to play the bad guy for the sake of the team! I—I *definitely* wasn't just in it for the delicious, delicious sweets!"

"………"

"Also, all I ever told him were the combinations. We screwed up that bathroom attack all on our own! It's not even worth getting mad over a betrayal that small!"

"………"

"And to quote one Ms. Erna: '*If you believe in anyone, you lose. That's what being a* spy *is all about.*' That's all there was to it!"

The others shared a glance. They were all thinking the same thing. *This girl has no shame.*

Now then, how best to punish the traitor…

"I've got an idea," the cerulean-haired girl offered. "Lily can be useful to us, right? The target still thinks she's on his side, so we can use that against him."

"Y-yeah! I can be like a double agent! See, now this really feels like spy train—"

"And there's no time like the present."

Lily's expression froze. "Uh, umm… I'm pretty sure this is gonna end with Teach beating me up…"

"Good luck!"

"C'mooon, there's gotta be a better way I can be of use. Look, I promise I won't betray you guys anymore, okay?"

"Time's a wastin'."

"…Yes ma'am." Lily's shoulders slumped as she left the main hall.

A short while later, they heard her upstairs.

"Teach! I just stole this from the others, and you're gonna want to see this! It has their plan all laid out; come take a look. There you go, closer, closer… Ha-ha! You're wide open! Now, prepare to—GAH! You got paint all over my maidenly nose!"

It sounded like the traitor had learned her lesson.

The girls nodded in satisfaction.

"Yo, Erna!"

The pink-haired girl leaped up with a purehearted look in her eyes and rushed over to Erna. She squeezed Erna's hand in delight and pressed her face right next to hers.

Erna shrank back from her innocent smile. "Y-yes…?"

"You're amazing!"

For a moment, Erna stared at her in shock.

When she looked up, she discovered that the rest of the team was smiling warmly at her as well.

Erna resisted the urge to cry. "…Of course I am," she replied in a show of false bravado.

◇◇◇

Later, Erna paid a visit to Klaus's room.

Lily had been tied up with string and left on the ground. Sure enough, Klaus had completely turned the tables on her.

"Erna." Still facing his canvas, Klaus spoke. "Would you mind taking out the trash for me? She stirs up a fuss whenever I try to move her."

Erna did as instructed and rolled Lily across the room.

Lily expressed her objections with a look of desperation on her face. "Teach, I'm begging you! I'll do anything! If I can't have your financiers anymore, I'm afraid I'm going to lose my—"

"You're betraying us again?!" Erna cried.

Klaus shooed her away with his hand. "Get her out of here."

Erna was glad to do so and rolled Lily all the way out of the room.

"You didn't put drugs in those sweets, did you?"

"Of course not." Klaus was holding out a plate to her.

The buttery financiers atop it gleamed like jewels.

"Would you like one? I happen to be in the market for a new master key."

"No."

"They're freshly baked…"

He brought the dish right up to Erna's nose. She could smell the financiers' sugary aroma, and before she realized it, she had already stuffed one in her mouth. It crumbled on her tongue, filling her mouth with a full-bodied sweetness.

"My friends are dead to me."

"I was kidding." Klaus handed her the whole plate and told her to share with the others. "I can't throw too many curveballs, or it'll make for poor training."

Klaus sometimes came off cold and robotic, so it was surprising to see he had so many hobbies. Between chess, cooking, and painting, he was a jack-of-all-trades.

Erna stepped closer to Klaus to get a look at the painting he was working on. He didn't seem to be making any progress on his messy scrawl of red paint.

Down in the bottom right, she could see the word *Family*.

"Teach, aren't you going to finish it…?"

"A fair question… I bought all this new paint, but my brush won't seem to move."

She could see the pathos in Klaus's eyes.

She hadn't known him for long, but over the course of their round-the-clock attacks and counterattacks, she had slowly developed a sense for the subtleties in his emotions.

"Was your family the ones who lived here before us…?"

Klaus's breath caught in his throat. It was rare to see him so visibly surprised. "I didn't think you'd figure it out so quickly."

"There were all sorts of little clues."

"How much were you able to deduce?" Klaus crossed his legs and turned his gaze straight toward her.

Erna explained her reasoning, breaking down her logic point by point. "There were people who lived at Heat Haze Palace before us. It stood to reason that you were a member of that spy team. But given that they aren't here anymore, the team must have disbanded—or was possibly wiped out. If I had to guess, I imagine the Impossible Mission Lamplight is going on is—"

"Very well. That's enough." Klaus cut her off and nodded. "By and large, your assumptions were on the mark. But the time isn't right for me to elaborate."

"Hmm...?"

"Don't worry. In twenty days, I'll reveal everything. And when I do, I'm sure you will all understand."

Why wait twenty days? As Erna began to wonder about that, though, Klaus went on, his tone firmer than ever.

"Then, it begins. Our long-awaited Impossible Mission."

Chapter 3

Intel Gathering

A girlish scream echoed through Heat Haze Palace.

That day, their attack had involved booby traps.

In fact, they'd packed the mansion to the brim with them. The idea was to have the target avoid the first trap, only to trigger the second, and then when he evaded that one, to trigger the third trap in turn. Imprisoned in a hellish labyrinth of unending wires, he would eventually fall—or at least, that was the plan. But Klaus hadn't just avoided the traps, he'd turned them back against them. Things ultimately devolved into a trap battle between Klaus and the girls, and Klaus emerged the overwhelming victor.

The girls needed to be able to detect one another's traps, so they left subtle ciphers around, but Klaus ended up rewriting all of them.

In the end, the members of Lamplight ended up in the main hall, bound head to toe in wire.

"Ahhhhhhh! Nothing works!"

The black-haired girl let out a hysterical cry at their unseemly defeat. She had come across as mature and elegant when they first arrived, but fatigue was taking a toll on her.

"Urgh, I never imagined I was *this* lacking... It's like our skills haven't grown a single bit!"

"That's not true at all." Klaus shook his head.

Normally, he would wound their pride by remarking "Your scheme was lacking," then finish them off with "That didn't even make for decent sport," but today was different.

He crossed his arms, then closed his eyes in admiration. "You've become strong. We're closing in on four weeks, and you've all shown dramatic growth since the day you arrived. The only reason you can't see it is because I'm simply too strong."

"…Really?"

"Really," Klaus agreed emphatically. "You've grown enough for me to trust you, if nothing else."

The girls looked at one another.

Klaus often called them magnificent during their attacks day in and day out, but to them, it came off as mockery. Although he doubtless meant it as a sincere compliment, those he was complimenting couldn't accept that sincerity.

This was the first time he had ever properly praised them, and a sense of accomplishment was finally sinking in.

"Now, it's high time I told you something." Klaus took a seat. "Allow me to explain why Lamplight was founded—as well as the details of our Impossible Mission."

"Not that I'm not *super*-curious about all that…" Lily cut him off. "But first, could you let us out of these wires?"

"Our job is to steal a sample of a bioweapon." He wasn't even listening.

When the girls pictured this all-important briefing, they hadn't expected to be completely bound while attending.

After coming to terms with their surreal situation, they gave Klaus their full attention.

He had mentioned something about stealing a bioweapon.

The white-haired girl coolly cut in. "Wait, don't international treaties ban the use of bioweapons?"

"Their use, yes, but not their development—or at least, that's how the meatheads over in our army chose to interpret the law when they forged ahead with their research. However, a sample was stolen by a Galgad spy. Our scientists estimate it will take them another year to actually analyze its structure, but we can't afford to be that optimistic. We need to retrieve that sample as soon as possible or, at the very least, destroy it."

"Ah." The girls sighed in understanding.

In this line of work, it was simply a fact of life that their country's military and its intelligence agency would work out of step. Everyone knew the military's top brass was spinning their wheels in a futile attempt to wash away the shame allowing their country to be invaded. The development of this bioweapon must have been one result of that.

No matter how skilled an intelligence agency was, it was impossible for them to know every little thing that went on inside their borders.

That was a weakness the Empire had exploited.

"B-by the way," the brown-haired girl asked timidly. "What's exactly *is* this bioweapon we're supposed to steal?"

"Would you like to see a picture from the lab?" Klaus withdrew a photograph from his pocket.

When the girls looked at it, not a single one of them could stop themselves from screaming.

The corpse was in such a horrific state that words seemed hardly sufficient to describe it. Given that they were bound and unable to flee, the experience was akin to torture.

"It's called Abyss Doll—a killer virus. It has a one-week incubation period during which it spreads through airborne droplets, and once symptoms show up, it kills within twelve hours. As a weapon, it's pure evil. And now it's fallen into the Empire's hands. These are people who have no qualms about murdering innocent civilians while carrying out assassinations. If it's ever used for subversive activities, Abyss Doll's casualty count would number in the six or seven figures. And if the military uses it, the world will come to an end."

Klaus gave his call to action.

"I trust you understand the responsibility we carry on our shoulders."

Millions of casualties—and if anything, that estimate was conservative.

In the previous war, the Empire had butchered civilians by the thousands, and they stopped at nothing to achieve their ends. If they unleashed this new weapon, then the Din Republic would no doubt retaliate in kind. With both sides spreading killer viruses left and right, everything would descend into hell on Earth. The girls couldn't even imagine the suffering that would ensue.

They gulped as it set in just how important their mission was.

"Now, this is a mission that was already attempted once before, by a team called Inferno."

"Inferno…?" The name elicited a reaction from the black-haired girl. "I've heard about them!"

"Oh? I didn't realize that information had leaked. Surprisingly sloppy of them."

"Not at all! They're the best spy team in the Republic!"

Her elegant, lilting manner of speech accelerated into a rapid-fire explanation of how Inferno was the ideal to which all spy teams in their nation aspired. How they had played a key role in protecting their country since even before the war. How the information they stole on the Imperial troops' movements helped evacuate hundreds of thousands of civilians. And how the misinformation they spread helped end the war by convincing the Empire's military leadership that victory was impossible.

Perhaps she had some connection to them herself, as she seemed oddly well-informed.

"When I became a spy, it was because I wanted to join Inferno!" she announced, finishing her speech.

Despite her passion, however, Klaus was as collected as ever. "Unfortunately," he replied coldly, "Inferno was wiped out."

"Huh?"

"They all died during their mission to retrieve Abyss Doll."

The black-haired girl's lip quivered. "It can't be…"

"To be more accurate, there was one survivor. The one person who was on a separate mission at the time—*me*." Then, to make himself perfectly clear, Klaus added, "I used to be a member of Inferno."

Now the girls knew who Klaus truly was.

He was a member of their country's best and brightest spy team.

None of them were particularly surprised, given his skills.

"That concludes my explanation. Our mission is to take the fate of our nation on our shoulders and succeed where Inferno failed. Nothing more, nothing less."

Klaus went silent. He had said all that needed saying.

None of the girls uttered a word. They certainly hadn't been taking their training lightly, but now that they knew the stark reality of their situation, their limbs felt like ice.

A band of washouts had to take on a mission that a group of elite spies had failed.

Every instinct in their bodies was screaming in terror. That 90 percent mortality rate weighed on them heavier than ever.

But they couldn't flee, either. The image of that grisly corpse had been seared into their brains. If they didn't do this, countless innocent civilians would—

"If you want out, that's fine," Klaus said as their anxiety reached a fever pitch.

Their eyes went wide. That wasn't what they'd been expecting.

"This isn't your problem. Yes, I'm here for revenge, but even the lives of millions of your countrymen doesn't mean you should have to risk yours. This is Din's problem as well as mine. Of course, there is a reason I chose you all. I do want you to come. But you don't have to. I can't force you to undertake a mission this harsh merely for the sake of your country."

Klaus looked at the girls.

"I'm giving you the day off. Use it to decide for yourselves if you're coming."

He waved his arm, and the wires binding the girls came undone. He turned, heading back toward his room. This discussion was over, for now.

The girls had enough to grapple with just taking it all in. They had been given a huge amount of information—the Impossible Mission's details, Klaus's identity, the demise of their nation's best team—and they needed to process it. None of them moved. They simply blinked.

Then, one of them broke the silence.

"I'm in."

It was Lily.

Klaus stopped in his tracks and turned back around. "Well, that's a surprise. I wouldn't have guessed you'd be the first to decide."

"Eh, I figured I wouldn't change my mind either way." She bashfully rubbed the back of her neck. "What about you guys?"

When the girls all looked at one another, they broke into grins. Nobody voiced any objections.

Not a single one of them needed time to think it over.

"All seven of you will be participating, then?" Klaus asked once more.

The members of Lamplight nodded and met Klaus's gaze with determination in their eyes.

Klaus replied with a small nod of his own. "Magnificent. Let's make sure we all come back alive."

Klaus sat in front of the canvas in his room.

"............................"

This was his routine.

Other than the time he spent working, training, and dealing with the girls, he had allotted his entire schedule to oil painting, yet he still hadn't made a lick of progress. He would hold his brush aloft with every intention of painting yet be unable to lay down so much as a single stroke. Before he noticed, the brush's tip would dry out.

The reason he'd fallen into a slump was plain as day.

When he first heard that Inferno had been wiped out, he lost something important to him.

And now he couldn't make any progress on his painting.

There were two types of painters: those who painted on theory and those who painted on instinct. It went without saying that Klaus fell into the latter camp, and that meant he had few tools at his disposal for overcoming those setbacks. In fact, it was starting to throw him off in other areas of his life as well.

It was unusual for him to get so worked up—but that was a sign of just how much this mission meant to him.

This mission took my family from me...

He was an orphan. His earliest memories were of living in a poverty-stricken town. Shunned by even the other urchins, he was destined to fade away in solitude.

Then Guido met him and invited him to join Inferno.

"From now on, your name is Klaus. I'm gonna make you into a spy."

When he closed his eyes, he could still hear the things Guido had said to him all those years ago.

"You'll get a warm bed, three square meals, and hot baths. And most importantly—friends. The team and I will teach you every skill under the sun. Fair warning, some of 'em can be a bit rough. They're all kinda oddballs, but they're good folk. Someday, you'll think of 'em as family."

And Guido had been right.

To Klaus, the people he had lived with here at Heat Haze Palace were the only family he had.

I have to complete this mission, no matter what it takes...

He reminisced as though slowly flipping through a hefty tome of memories, getting more sentimental with each page he turned.

After a little while in that reverie, he heard a knock on his door.

Before he could reply, Lily popped her head in.

"Hey, Teach, Teach! You got our battle plan drawn up yet?"

"More importantly..." Klaus stepped back from his canvas. "Are you sure about this? When we first met, you made it abundantly clear how badly you want to avoid dying. I thought you would at least take more time to make up your mind."

"Wait, now I'm the one getting questioned?"

An expression of shock crossed Lily's face as she flopped down into a chair.

Lately, the girls had become more relaxed around Klaus. It was hard to stay stiff and proper around someone when you spent half your waking hours attacking him with a knife.

"Hmm... Y'know, I don't know how well I can explain it, but..." Lily scratched her cheek. "...You promise not to be too surprised, Teach?"

"About what?"

"Well, the truth is: I'm actually a pretty self-centered person."

"Sure, but what's the surprise?"

"So back at school, I was all like *I wanna do great!* and *I want everyone to think I'm awesome!* but I never really thought through any of it. I didn't have any real *goals*, y'know? And even here, I was super-psyched about getting to be the team's leader, but at first, that was all there was to it." Lily looked at the ceiling as her voice dropped to a murmur. "But lately, I've kinda started wanting to become a better leader for the sake of the team."

"Oh?"

Now that *was* a surprise.

Klaus had made sure not to intrude on the girls' personal lives any more than he had to, so her heart must have started to shift without him even noticing.

Before he could admire her too much, though, her whole body shivered.

"Man, whenever I spend more than thirty seconds talking seriously, I start feeling itchy all over."

"That has concerning implications about your personality."

"Anyway, I said I'm going, so that's that. It's a bit late to be asking me about it, honestly. And kinda insensitive." Lily acted playfully embarrassed to try to change the subject—although the blush on her cheeks revealed that her embarrassment was genuine.

"...No, you're right. What's important now is the plan."

His very first student was showing some admirable growth.

Klaus raised both his index fingers, then bent them one after the other as he spoke.

"You will all be infiltrating the research facility from the east. I'll be doing the same from the west."

"Aye, aye, captain."

He avoided giving any details, instead choosing to outline the plan in broad strokes.

"In the days before the operation, we'll be spending our time gathering intel. I'm counting on you, *Leader*."

That was exactly what Lily had been hoping to hear.

She rushed out of the room, murmuring to herself with great delight. "It's time for Wunderkind Lily's big debut!"

$$\diamond\diamond\diamond$$

One week later, all of Lamplight's members left Heat Haze Palace.

In order to best infiltrate the Galgad Empire, the team split up into two groups. Klaus and several of the girls obtained work visas by posing as artists, and Lily and the rest got tourist visas as rich young ladies who were coming to enjoy the Empire's performing arts. It went without saying that all their passports were fakes.

When they got to the customs stations, they were subjected to harsh questioning about the reasons for their visit and the places they intended to stay. Their opposition was twofold: the immigrations officers doing the actual questioning and the soldiers standing behind them keeping a watchful eye on the proceedings. The Empire had no desire to let spies into their borders. All of their luggage was thoroughly inspected as well, and without the fake backstories they'd practiced and practiced ahead of time, they would have gotten arrested on the spot.

Half a day later, though, they were all across the border, and everything after that went so smoothly, it was almost anticlimactic.

Nobody seemed to be tailing them, and they were able to purchase train tickets without any fuss. In fact, the attendant at the ticket window was downright friendly to them.

The girls thought back to Klaus's lectures.

As far as what they were supposed to do after entering the country went—

"Just walk casually, and you won't have anything to worry about."

—his instruction had been perfunctory at best.

When the girls complained, he racked his brains to give them a proper explanation.

"The thing is: It's trivial to blend in once you're actually inside the country. You only need to worry after you start interacting with the relevant parties, so there's no need to be on edge when you're just traveling."

"Why's it so easy...?"

"You probably don't realize it because you're so entrenched in the world of espionage, but as far as most people are concerned, the war is long over. Many of them still bear hatred toward enemy nations, but they don't think of themselves as currently being at war. After all, they have no way of knowing about all the battles happening in the spy world."

"Huh. When you put it that way, it's a little sad..."

"This is for the best. It's the whole reason behind our shadow war."

After crossing the border, the team boarded a train.

A family sat in the seats beside Lily's, all dressed in black. Maybe they'd just come from a funeral. Two children who appeared to be brothers were staring out the window with their faces pressed right up against the glass and their eyes gleaming.

As far as they knew, the world was at peace.

They lived their lives blissfully unaware of the things their nation's spies were doing. They had no idea that politicians were being bought off, gangs were being secretly funded, researchers were being threatened, and people were being murdered under the guise of accidents right under their noses.

In fact, they didn't even know that the people sitting next to them were a group of enemy operatives.

What an odd world this is, Lily mused.

And what odd creatures spies were...

As the thoughts quietly swam through her head, one of the boys from the next seat over peeled himself from the window and came running toward them.

"Hey, miss! Where are you all going?"

"Hmm? My friends and I are here to see a musical. I hear it's the talk of the Empire."

"Wow, cool! Where are you staying?"

"Hee-hee, aren't you a precocious little guy. You know, it's bad manners to ask a girl something like that."

As Lily sidestepped the boy's question, another thought crossed her mind.

It'd be nice to go on a trip with friends like this for real someday.

How great would it be if they could forget about the shadow war like this kid and just have a good time?

After they got to their station, Lily pretended to get lost and sat down on a bench.

As she and the other girls unfurled a map, a man sat down on the bench back-to-back with theirs.

"From here on, we'll be operating separately," he said without turning around. "Proceed according to plan. Do you have anything you need to say?"

"We'll have all the time in the world to chat next time we see each other," Lily replied.

"Very well."

The man left.

Lily and the others did the same and headed to their prearranged hotel.

With that, the Impossible Mission had well and truly begun.

The Endy Laboratory stood on the very edge of the Galgad Empire's capital.

As befitted a global metropolis, the Galgad capital was packed to the brim with high-rises. The tallest building in the Din Republic was their parliament at eight stories tall, while the Galgad capital was full of structures that casually dwarfed it. One peculiarity of Imperial architecture was that all their high-rises were steepled; the rows of black spires jutting into the sky evoked both awe and unease.

The city had served as the Empire's capital since the medieval era and had flourished ever since. The sea and mountains flanking it provided a great defense against invaders, and its tall steeples allowed the city to best make use of its limited real estate.

A thousand years of force and violence had enabled this pincushion of a city to prosper greatly, and the Endy Laboratory had been built on a cliff overlooking all of it.

The good news was that it was hard to miss.

The bad news was that the number of infiltration routes was limited.

This was the building Lamplight needed to infiltrate.

"The sample is somewhere in the Endy Laboratory. That was where our transmitters cut out, and there's no sign it's been moved."

They had held their strategy meeting in advance.

"Our objective is to sneak in and steal it."

"...Security will be tight, won't it?"

"It will. Although it's officially a branch laboratory for a legitimate pharmaceutical company, the facility's actual purpose is to develop cutting-edge weaponry, and they have military personnel stationed on-site as permanent guards. Our success or failure will be determined by how much intel we can gather ahead of time."

"Does it have any vulnerabilities...?"

"Of course. Anytime humans are running the show, there are going to be weaknesses. No matter who they are, everyone has to eat, everyone

has to shit, everyone has to bathe, everyone needs time off, and everyone likes to get laid sometimes. We aren't machines."

Then Klaus made his announcement to the girls.

"For this mission, I've divided you into three squads."

"Intel squad—your job is to coordinate with the other squads and gather as much information as possible."

The black-haired girl smiled gracefully as she thought back to Klaus's instructions.

It was nighttime, and she was sitting at a sidewalk café.

She had neglected her skin care regimen during their battles against Klaus, but after resuming it in preparation for the mission, she looked more radiant than ever.

She was the most attractive and physically mature member of the team, and she knew exactly how men saw her. Her outfit wasn't extravagant or flashy but trim and tidy to a T. She knew that the best way to attract men wasn't with an outfit that lay her skin bare but one that covered it and accentuated her body's natural curves. The dress she was wearing hugged her breasts just right.

She sat on the café's terrace and sipped her ice coffee. When she looked over her shoulder, she discovered that the bespectacled young man in the seat beside hers was glancing at her chest. Even after he looked away, he couldn't help but snatch another few peeks.

With that renewed confirmation of her own attractiveness, the black-haired girl smiled to herself. The self-confidence Klaus had all but shattered was back with a vengeance.

My first instinct is to try to make contact as soon as possible by spilling coffee on him, but...

She thought back to her battles against Klaus.

She had tried using fake apologies to start up conversations, but that was so heavy-handed that all it had done was put him on guard.

She wasn't going to make that same mistake here.

Instead, she just paid close attention and waited. Impatience would ruin everything. Whenever her actions were even a little bit off, Klaus saw through them in an instant. She needed to imagine her target as him.

She sat there for nearly twenty minutes, waiting for the perfect timing.

The best option isn't to spill my drink on him, *it's to get him to spill it on* me.

The moment the man stood up, she saw her opportunity and slid her cup over to the corner of the table, where the man's backpack smacked into it. Her glass toppled to the ground and loudly shattered, splashing coffee all over her dress.

"Oh, I'm so sorry! I'll pay you back for it!"

The man got even more flustered than she'd expected as he began gathering up the shards.

The black-haired girl grabbed his hand. "No, no. You mustn't pick up glass with your bare hands."

When she did, his face went bright red. He clearly didn't have much experience with women.

He was no match for her.

"Oh, forgive me. I—I didn't mean to grab your hand like that...," she apologized, putting on an innocent facade. "But...you have such nice fingers. Are you an artisan?"

"N-no, just a regular old researcher...," her target said falteringly, scratching his head in confusion.

"Wow! You must be really smart, then."

Between the guilt from breaking her glass and the exaltation of having a pretty girl touching him, his brain was having trouble keeping up.

The black-haired girl squeezed his hand to shatter the last of his defenses. "Hee-hee. This is a pretty expensive dress, mister. How are you going to apologize for staining it?"

"Um, er, I..."

"My date just stood me up, you know. How about you treat me to dinner?"

She smiled, and the man timidly nodded.

"Specialist squad—your job is to use your abilities to assist the other squads."

The blond girl—Erna—hummed to herself as she strolled down a road on the capital's outskirts.

Night had fallen, and it had just begun to rain. Although the moon hung high in the sky, the road Erna was on was nearly pitch-black. She could barely see a foot or two in front of her, and on more than one occasion, she came dangerously close to tripping. It had also gotten chilly, so she had to warm her hands up with her breath. She was surrounded on all sides by fields, with nary a house to be seen anywhere.

Then, an oncoming car's headlights cleaved through the darkness across from her.

Erna sniffed the air, and after confirming there was no danger around her, leaped out in front of it.

As the driver's scream and the car's horn cut through the air, Erna gently flopped onto the ground.

The car came to an abrupt stop, and a woman rushed out. "A-are you okay?"

Erna suddenly realized that her clothes didn't look dirty enough, so she surreptitiously smeared her skirt with mud. She then pretended to cry.

"I-I'm so scaaared... I went for a long walk, and then all of a sudden, it was dark, and then a car showed up out of nowhere..."

Flustered, the woman offered to give Erna a ride home. The young operative got in the back seat, and the woman set off. She clearly was sorry for the mud-covered girl. Erna felt bad about manipulating her, but this was no time to be worrying about things like that.

"Oh, that right turn there!" Erna guided her. The woman yanked her steering wheel.

When she did, the car ran straight into a pool of mud on the side of the road.

Its right wheel lurched, then came to a stop.

The roads that far from the city center were poorly serviced, so these things happened all the time when it rained.

The woman pressed on the gas pedal a couple times, then scratched her head. "I have to get out to push the car. Would you mind holding the wheel for me?" she asked.

When her target got out, Erna moved up to the front. Maintaining her cool nonchalance, she fiddled with the seat and grabbed hold of the envelope in its hidden compartment. As she did, the car came free of the mud.

From there, she had the woman drop her off on a corner in a residential area. "Thank you so much, miss!" she said as she vigorously waved and watched the woman go.

Once the car was gone from view, another girl slunk out from behind the houses.

The second girl had brown hair, and she observed Erna with even greater concern than usual on her often-anxious face. When her faltering gaze landed on the envelope Erna was holding, she let out an impressed cry.

The uncharacteristic smile vanished off Erna's face and was replaced with the cold eyes of a spy as she offered her contact the stolen envelope. "Get this to the Intel squad as quickly as possible."

"Out of curiosity, what is it?"

"That lady is a Din Republic informant, and she's been passing us valuable information for years. But now…"

Erna opened the envelope.

Inside, there were instructions from the Imperial army.

"…She's switched sides to the Empire. If we'd taken her intel at face value, we could've been in serious trouble."

"Wow, yikes. I felt bad for doubting an ally, but it looks like I was right to."

"No, that was excellent. I think it's good for a spy to be a bit of a coward."

"Well, we did have a teammate who betrayed us for a few sweets…" The brown-haired girl smiled bashfully, then whistled through her fingers. "All right, all set for delivery. As long as they're within five miles, they'll have it within ten minutes."

As Erna looked at her quizzically, a hawk swooped down toward them and slammed straight into Erna's face. With a quiet "How unlucky…" she keeled over backward.

The hawk then took the envelope and quickly vanished into the sky at fifty miles per hour.

"Operations squad—your job is to exploit the data the Intel squad gathers and use it to interact with key individuals."

A white-haired girl walked briskly down the city's main drag. She kept her head low so as not to be noticed, shooting keen glances around her as she went.

It was nearing noon, and the streets were packed with workers taking their lunch breaks. The white-haired girl wove her way through the crowd, waiting for the perfect timing to pass by her target.

Meanwhile, the silver-haired girl beside her—Lily—bemoaned her empty stomach. "I could sure go for some lunch…"

"We can eat later," the white-haired girl shot back in exasperation. As she did, a brawny man started coming toward them from the other direction. That was their guy.

When the white-haired girl began fretting over when to give Lily the signal, she suddenly heard a comical growling sound coming from Lily's stomach. She must have been ravenous. Lily tottered unsteadily across the sidewalk—

"Yeep!"

—then crashed right into their target.

"The hell's your problem?!" the man roared.

He was far heavier than Lily, and she tumbled to the ground the moment she slammed into him. She pressed down on her head. "I-I'm sorry!"

The people around them watched the exchange with concern, but the man had had enough of their stares. He clicked his tongue and kept moving.

Lily let out a big sigh. "Yeesh, that was scary."

"More subtle next time." The white-haired girl flicked Lily right in the forehead.

"Ow! …So?"

"Got it."

The white-haired girl grinned and flashed her the inside of the bag slung over her shoulder. The man's wallet sat inside. She had picked his pocket while his attention was focused on Lily.

"Just to be sure, that's the real one, right?"

"Duh. You really think a dummy wallet's gonna fool me?"

"Teach fooled you with dummies fourteen times."

"Yeah, and now I know better. When you crashed into that guy, the wallet he immediately reached for was the one by his chest, not the one in his back pocket. That means this one's the real deal."

The two of them headed away from the main road and began making their way down a side alley.

"Let's get back to the hotel and rip this sucker open," the white-haired girl said. "The big guy back there was a drug dealer, and his wallet's got a list of his clients in it. If Intel is right, some of his buyers work at the lab."

"I'm looking forward to dropping that anonymous tip."

"Yeah, once we've wrung 'em for all they're good for."

Lily let out a pleased hum. "You know, I was kinda worried at first, but we've come a long way, haven't we?"

"Yeah, and no wonder. Even if it was just a month of training like that—"

But right as the two of them turned to each other and smirked—

"You two! Stop right there!"

—they heard a sharp call from behind them.

They turned around, then let out quiet groans. It was a spy's natural enemy—the police.

A pair of male officers blocked their escape route.

"Don't move. We need to see what's in your bag."

"Uh, we're just regular old tourists, though…"

"Sorry, but we've had a rash of pickpockets around these parts. We hope you don't mind cooperating."

The white-haired girl's coolheaded deflection ended in failure.

"Why'd you pick somewhere that has a pickpocketing problem?" Lily whispered to her.

"Because you wanted to get lunch afterward," the white-haired girl shot back with a glare.

If worse came to worst, they could take the officers down, but that would cause all sorts of problems. That had to be an absolute last resort.

The white-haired girl obediently handed the bag over.

The officer snatched it from her hand, then stabbed it without so much as hesitating. The bag's false bottom wasn't going to do them any good. In mere moments, the officer would find a wallet containing somebody else's ID.

Now then, how were they going to lie their way out of this one…?

"All right, looks like we're all good."

Despite their fears, the officer quickly ended the search. He never found the wallet in the bag or on their persons.

Once the officers were gone, Lily cocked her head to the side. "So where'd you hide the wallet?"

"I dunno."

"Huh?"

"It's gone." The white-haired girl seemed vexed. "Someone stole the wallet I stole—and there's only one guy I know who could pull that off."

She thought back—and then she remembered the last thing Klaus had said after splitting them up into their squads.

"And as for me—I'll be focused on providing you backup."

Right then, a man strolled past them.

He was dressed in a lovely suit, and by all accounts, he was a typical elderly gentleman. The disguise was perfect. He lifted his lapel ever so slightly and revealed the wallet inside so only the girls could see. With a look of utter nonchalance on his face, he exited the alleyway.

Not everything went perfectly.

All in all, though, the Lamplight girls did a damn fine job.

For interested readers, the exact details of their plan were decided as follows.

"As far as specifics go, the Intel squad should make like a rose sweetly blooming, the Operations squad should zoop-zoop-zoop *around, and the Specialist squad should watch over them like they would a baby bird—"*

"......................."

When he felt the girls staring icily at him, Klaus cut himself off.

"—I was joking."

Not a single one of them laughed, but they did breathe deep sighs of relief. They didn't know what they'd have done had he been serious.

"Actually, the details are yours to decide."

He cast a gentle gaze across the group.

"I'll provide overarching direction and check-in regularly, but I'm leaving the specifics in your hands."

"Are...are you sure?"

"You're ready, aren't you? It's what you've been doing for the past month."

His words were meant to spur them into action—and they achieved just that.

The team glanced at one another, and an elegant smile spread across the black-haired girl's face.

"Don't you worry about a thing. We'll come up with a plan so perfect it will knock your socks off."

"Magnificent."

That was their signal. The girls spread a map out across the table.

How were they going to deceive their foes? Who should be the ones to approach each target?

Whenever one of the girls offered up an idea, another one would find a hole in it, a third would come up with an amended proposal, and a fourth would argue with that. The most common retort offered was *"That didn't work against Teach."* Many of the initial proposals suggested were ones that had already failed against Klaus, so they all worked together to make them craftier.

They were driven by a single goal—come up with plans good enough to fool Teach!

That was the fruit of their month of labor.

One night, as Klaus sat in his hotel room reading the newspaper, he heard a knock.

"I have the wine you ordered."

He opened the door. One of the hotel's bellhops stood outside.

He invited the bellhop in and turned on the room's record player. That would prevent any potential listening devices from being able to make out their conversation.

The bellhop let out a deep sigh, then reached up and appeared to tear his face off, although it was just a mask. Underneath were a pair of gentle eyes and a face that seemed somehow transient. They belonged to the red-haired girl, who was a member of the Intel squad.

"It's an excellent disguise," Klaus said as he took the wine from her, "but there really was no need for you to take off the mask, was there?"

"But I don't like cross-dressing around you, Boss..."

"...I'm not complaining; I'm just saying."

He got the feeling that the girl might hold an unusual amount of affection toward him.

Rather than investigate the matter further, though, he simply told her not to call him Boss.

He peeled the wine's label off and looked at the coded message on its backside. It contained the intel the girls had managed to dig up. One glance was enough to tell him just how hard they were working.

The red-haired girl gave him a modest bow.

"We've confirmed that Abyss Doll is still in the laboratory, but... infiltrating it is going to be a challenge. It's out in the middle of nowhere, and its surroundings are under constant surveillance. Also, only a small number of people hold the keys to the deepest parts of the lab, so we won't be able to get into those areas even if we use disguises to sneak into the building. Our only option is to break in, but we need more time to—"

"No. If we take any more time, the Empire will finish analyzing the sample. We can't put this off."

"But..."

"I haven't been slacking, either, you know." Klaus lifted up the room's bed.

A huge quantity of documents and IDs had been sewn to its underside. There were enough of them to cover the whole mattress, and they included everything from criminal records of laboratory personnel, details on their families, blueprints from when the lab's buildings were first constructed, lists of politicians who had ties to the facility, military personnel records, and even the Galgad Ministry of Finance's budget documents on the lab.

"You did all this on your own...?"

The red-haired girl blinked. After quickly skimming through the documents, she let out a deep sigh and looked at Klaus with eyes full of wonder.

"This is amazing. It's so heartening, watching an expert work."

"An expert, huh…? I suppose so. As the Greatest Spy in the World, this was child's play, but—"

Klaus paused. He looked at the ceiling, then closed his eyes.

"—would you mind giving me a moment?"

The red-haired girl blinked again.

Klaus headed out into the darkened city.

This particular excursion hadn't been planned, but here he was. If asked why he'd gone out, his only answer would have been *I just felt like it*. Explaining the reasoning behind his actions wasn't exactly his strong suit.

In all likelihood, the real reason was that he had gotten anxious.

…I'm not perfect. Certainly not the way I let them think I am.

Everything he could do now was entirely thanks to the harsh training Inferno had put him through.

When he'd first joined Inferno, he'd had even less polish than the girls did now. It was only after a group of the finest spies in the nation personally taught him that he had become the person he was now. And during those days of intense training, he had failed constantly.

Guido's lessons, in particular, had ended with him flat on his face more times than he could count.

"Your fighting's shit. You don't have what it takes to beat me."

No matter how hard he'd tried, he could never match up to his mentor.

Each time Klaus tried to strike him, he'd found himself flying through the air, and Guido blocked even his strongest punches with ease.

"You're a tenth of a second too slow—and you always will be."

"You really gotta ask the others for lessons every now and again. Learn about negotiation and disguises and stuff. Fighting ain't even a core spy skill."

"You already learned everything else by intuition? Learn some theory, dumbass."

"You're gonna end up teaching others someday, you know. You want your students to end up dead?"

"You're not interested in teaching? Haaah... Fine. Then I'll keep beating you up till you've had enough."

Klaus never defeated him.

They sparred hundreds of times, but Klaus lost each and every one.

I never could close that tenth-of-a-second gap... I'm no expert. I'm barely less of an amateur than them.

Klaus arrived at the park and sat down by the edge of its fountain.

Due to the late hour, the park was full of people returning home from parties. They hummed to themselves with flush faces, enjoying life to the fullest. Klaus could tell there was still at least one party going on in the capital somewhere, as he could hear a violin playing off in the distance.

He focused on the sound of running water coming from behind him and closed his eyes.

"Hey there, good-looking. Three bills will buy you a round with me. What do you say?"

He opened them back up.

It sounded like a prostitute. Perhaps she'd mistaken him for a lonely bachelor.

When he looked in the direction of the voice, he found Erna swaying her body from side to side.

"...I'm not looking to buy."

"But if you don't, it'll ruin my 'exchange information by pretending to be a hooker' plan."

"I think you should come up with a different plan."

As far as bad moves went, anything liable to get her arrested was pretty high up on the list.

Undeterred, Erna sat down beside him. Klaus tried to shift over to at least put some space between them, but she followed him every step of the way.

"...Even if you want to pretend we're strangers who just happened to meet, spies need to avoid publicly interacting whenever possible. Why do you think I put the Intel squad in charge of communications?"

Despite his quiet reprimand, Erna showed no signs of moving away.

"What I'm delivering can't be passed on in a secret message."

"And what's that?"

"Love and affection."

What in the world was she talking about?

He considered asking that out loud but decided not to risk hurting her feelings.

"Are you…worried?" Erna turned her concerned gaze toward him.

Her words rang a hair too true, and her round, doll-like eyes watered. She had seen the wavering in his heart.

He didn't love the prospect of confiding his emotions to his subordinate, but he didn't want to spurn her kindness, either.

"Before I tell you that…I should tell you my real age."

"I'll admit, I am a bit curious."

"It's as you can see."

"So you *are* twenty-eight!"

"…Twenty, actually." Klaus was used to being seen as older than he was. It didn't hurt his feelings. Nuh-uh.

"…You're a lot younger than I thought," Erna remarked in amazement.

The oldest members of Lamplight were eighteen, so he was only two years separated from his subordinates.

"And as such, I have the same worries anyone my age would have. This is my first time being responsible for other people's lives. Not that I haven't put my own life on the line a fair few times, mind you."

"……"

"I know it's pathetic, but…it scares me, imagining how my own inexperience could get one of my subordinates killed."

He couldn't afford to show this weakness around the other girls. He could barely stand to show it to himself.

Erna gently laid her hand atop Klaus's.

"I'm not good at talking… So I can't come up with anything nice to say…" Her clear gaze was focused entirely on him. "So instead…I'll just hold your hand until the worries go away."

He was well past the age where holding his hand would be enough to calm his nerves, but the warmth from her touch conveyed just how earnest her feelings were.

He felt his heart lighten a little.

When he told her so, Erna gave him a satisfied smile and headed back the way she came.

The next evening, Klaus was in his hotel room writing out a coded message when he heard a knock on his door. He looked at the clock. It was nine o'clock sharp. Every day, she arrived at exactly the specified time. Klaus turned on the record player to counteract any potential bugs.

Then, he heard the red-haired girl's gentle voice from the other side of the door.

"Boss, I have the wine you ordered…"

Klaus nearly dropped his pen. He marched over to the door and was greeted by the serene smile of the red-haired girl in her male disguise.

He quickly ushered her inside. As she took off her mask, Klaus shot her an icy look.

"Don't go calling me Boss outside the room. It defeats the entire purpose of the disguise."

"Right. Sorry, Boss…"

"And don't call me Boss inside, either. If you don't like Teach, just Klaus is fine, too."

The red-haired girl looked down. "But I want to call you Boss, Boss…"

"Stubborn to the end, I see."

If she cared that much, Klaus had no choice but to fold. His dislike of the moniker was his problem, not hers.

By the time she finished giving her usual report, the red-haired girl was back to her normal, modest self. "There's one other thing, if you don't mind."

"What?"

"Lily asked me for a favor. She wants to have a party the evening before the mission for good luck."

"………"

Surely she must be joking.

Klaus squeezed the bridge of his nose.

"...Boss?"

"Sorry, I must have misheard. Did you say a party? She wants to have an entire group of undercover agents get together for a dinner?"

"That is what she said, yes."

"I really wish you'd just turned her down..."

He'd never so much as heard of spies holding a gathering like that. If even a single one of them got tailed, they would all be exposed.

The whole point was that even if one of them got made, the rest of the team could still carry out the mission without them. Getting together would defeat the entire purpose.

"You need to talk her out of it. It's unheard-of."

"I think she's already made a reservation at a fancy restaurant, though..."

"That girl doesn't have an ounce of shame in her body, does she?"

"I think she's worried the group is getting worn down."

That was a fair point.

Unlike him, for the girls, this was their first real mission. It made sense that exhaustion was taking its toll on them.

Even the red-haired girl's voice lacked vigor, and she had made the amateur mistake of calling him the wrong name before entering the room.

"...Fine, do what you want. I'll tell you the name of a restaurant with ties to our intelligence community. Make absolutely sure you don't get tailed."

The red-haired girl shook her head slightly at his concession.

"With just us, I'm a little concerned that something might go wrong..."

"Then don't do it."

"But if you came, too, that wouldn't be a problem..."

"........."

What, was he supposed to be their personal bodyguard or something?

However, she did have a point. At the end of the day, that was probably the best option.

"...I guess looking out for my subordinates is part of the job description." He exhaled with exasperation and covered his face with his hand. "I'll handle the reservation. And I suppose I'd better do some reconnaissance, too…"

The red-haired girl replied by giving him a deep bow.

The term *spy* contained a wide variety of different subcategories.

Although there were certainly some like Klaus and the girls who worked directly with their government, there were also informants who lived in foreign countries who got paid each time they passed along information, as well as sleeper agents who simply lived in those countries as regular citizens during peacetime.

The spot Klaus had selected for their party was a restaurant whose proprietor held the Empire in low regard. Although the owner didn't engage in any espionage directly, they had no interest in reporting Klaus's comings and goings to the authorities, either.

Klaus had reserved them a private room there.

He himself arrived a little bit late, as he first had to ensure that there weren't any tails and that the owner hadn't turned on them. He was still decidedly dubious that any party could be worth the labor that this one required.

The moment he entered the room, Lily gave him a big wave. "Hey there, stranger!"

"…Lily, do you have anything you'd like to say to me for letting you carry out this harebrained scheme of yours?"

"…You're welcome?"

Klaus silently flicked her in the forehead. "My skull!" she cried.

Klaus sat down, then glanced around at the girls' faces. It had been two weeks since he'd last seen them, and their expressions were visibly tenser, although their youthful innocence still leaked through.

When the food arrived, the festivities got rolling in earnest.

As always, Lily was at the center of the action. "Y'know, now that I think about it, I've kinda been killing it. Who'da thunk I'd do this well on my very first mission?!"

Predictably enough, her conceit earned her a good heckling from the other girls.

The first to pile on were her fellow Operations squad members.

"You spent half the time getting lost!" complained the cool white-haired girl, while her arrogant, cerulean-haired partner added, "And the other half sending me out to look for stuff you dropped."

By the sound of it, it was fortunate Lily had good people watching her back. As had become custom for the group, Lily's self-aggrandizing nonsense and the other girls' wry retorts helped keep the conversation lively.

Klaus elected not to join in, instead eating his food in silence.

I didn't realize it would get this noisy with all of them in one place. He frowned.

Meanwhile, one of the others came over to him.

"Teach," said Erna. After slicing up her lamb steak, she stabbed a piece with her fork and offered it to him. "Say aah."

The others let out cheers of delight.

"You go, girl!" "Yeah! Show him how manly you are!" "My, how aggressive…"

Klaus felt a headache coming on.

He felt for Erna but ignored the proffered fork.

"…Why aren't any of you nervous?" Klaus glared at the girls. "Do you really understand the situation we're in?"

Much as he was loath to give it, they needed a lecture.

This was no picnic they were on. They were heading into a life-or-death mission with millions of civilian lives on the line.

Now was no time to be letting their guard down.

It was the first time he had ever properly scolded them.

"………"

Lamplight all went silent. You could hear a pin drop.

He was worried he'd sunk their spirits. However, that wasn't the case.

The white-haired girl glared back at him. "Nervous? Of course I'm nervous. How could I not be? I'm scared stiff. Hell, my legs have been trembling since the minute we left Din."

"Then, why?"

"'*Cause* now you're here with us," she said, pursing her lips. "Right now, I figure we might just be okay. Your strength is the one thing I can count on."

Her companions nodded to signal their agreement.

Even so, they should have been more on guard. Klaus was tempted to chastise them further but decided to swallow his words.

It made sense now. The only reason they had looked carefree to him was because he was by their side. It would seem that a month straight of being bested by him had inflated his worth in their minds.

Klaus approached the white-haired girl.

"Wh-what…?" she asked, bracing herself.

"Here, your turn." Klaus held out the fork he'd stolen from Erna. "Say aah."

The white-haired girl's face flushed bright red. "What—? You—I… What the hell do you think you're doing?"

"If that's enough to shake you, I would reconsider that sense of security you feel."

Klaus gave his victim's forehead a flick, and the room erupted in laughter once more. He then offered the meat that the white-haired girl had rejected to Erna, who gleefully swallowed it down. For some reason, that earned her a round of applause from the others.

Luckily, Klaus was able to avoid spoiling the mood. Before long, it was just as clamorous as before.

Out of the blue, Lily made a comment. "Y'know, this is actually a first."

"A first what?"

"The first time you've joined us for dinner, Teach. You should eat with us more often."

"………"

It was a fair point.

Back at Heat Haze Palace, the girls all cooked together, whereas Klaus prepared his meals on his own. It wasn't particularly efficient, all things considered, but he had been taking the arrangement for granted.

Meals were something you ate with your family. Since Klaus had lost his, eating alone simply made sense to him.

Perhaps that was something he needed to loosen up on.

Klaus silently left the room.

After returning from the bathroom, Klaus was greeted by an unexpected sight.

All the girls were slumped over on the table.

Had they been attacked? Klaus glanced around to get a handle on the situation.

When he got closer, though, he realized they were breathing peacefully. There were no traces of gas in the air, no signs they'd been injected with anything, and no poison in the food. They had simply fallen asleep from partying themselves out.

The team had been working ceaselessly day and night, and it had been a month and two weeks since any of them had had a proper day off. The relief of finally being reunited with their friends and allies must have uncorked their pent-up exhaustion.

Even so, it takes a lot of nerve, falling asleep here and now of all times.

He reached over to shake them awake—but then decided not to.

There was no need to wake them up. Better to let them rest.

Even if they were ambushed, he could just fend off the attacker on his own.

I could tell myself this is all part of being in charge…but I'm not sure I'd believe myself.

When the waitress came over to deliver their post-meal coffee, Klaus asked if he could pay extra to extend their reservation. He didn't want to use official Lamplight funds for something like that, so the money came out of his own pocket. The waitress smiled happily as she looked at the comfy scene inside the room and readily agreed.

These girls… If they knew half the worry they cause me…

He looked at their sleeping faces and took a small breath.

Something his boss had once said flashed back through his mind.

"When someone lets you watch them sleep, that's how you know they really trust you. Those are the people you have to protect, no matter what."

Back when Klaus was much younger, he had dozed off in Heat Haze Palace's main hall, worn-out from his constant training. When he woke up, he discovered that the boss and the rest of Inferno were gathered around him, chuckling.

"Wait, Boss… Ain't it part of our job to wait for our enemies to let us catch 'em sleeping so we can do 'em in?"

"Come on, Guido. Don't say stuff like that in front of the kid."

"He's not a kid, Boss." Guido had clapped Klaus on the back. *"He's a*

prodigy. And when he grows up, this bastard's gonna be a better spy than any of us."

"Well, for now, he's still a kid. An adorable kid who nods off in the middle of the day."

Klaus had resisted the kindness. *"I'm...I'm not a kid."*

He'd been at that tender age when he was still a boy but wanted to be seen as a man.

The boss burst into laughter, and the rest of the team followed suit. Guido rapped Klaus on the head. *"Hey, he's got a mouth on him!"*

"This is a violence-free household," the boss had scolded, to which Guido fired back, *"No, it isn't; we're spies."* Klaus had smiled at the heartwarming exchange.

He was deep into reminiscing when a question suddenly occurred to him.

...Hmm? Why is it that I looked at them and immediately thought of Inferno?

The two teams were nothing alike.

One was a band of elite spies, and the other was a slapped-together group of amateurs. The two were as different as diamonds and gravel.

Regardless...it feels like their resolve is firm.

Klaus took another look at the girls. They were all resting peacefully, and Lily was even leaving a puddle of drool on the tablecloth.

He had to protect them, no matter what.

They were a bit of a handful, but that didn't matter.

If they believed in him, he would have to put his faith in the choice he had made, too.

Lily opened her eyes with a start.

Her cheek was wet. Had somebody pranked her? Did they get her while she was asleep? Clearly, revenge was in order.

She shook her head to clear away her drowsiness and wake herself up. When she did, she realized the situation she was in. She was still at the restaurant, but the table had been cleared, and her teammates were all asleep. They must have dozed off during the party.

"Ack! This is bad!" Lily leaped to her feet.

She could remember clearly how displeased Klaus had looked when he was pointing out how lax they were being. The fact that he so rarely scolded them only made their current blunder all the more egregious.

She frantically clapped her sleeping teammates on their backs.

"Up, up, up! If you keep sleeping, Teach is gonna pour olive oil up our noses!"

"I'm going to do what?" Klaus shot her a concerned look from the corner of the room where he was sipping his coffee.

Thanks to Lily, the other girls started waking up and fearing the wrath of Klaus. They had been determined to get their acts together but had succumbed to their drowsiness all the same.

However, Klaus reacted with utter calm.

In fact, this was the gentlest they had ever seen him look. He was even smiling, albeit only slightly.

"There's been a change to the plan. I originally said that you all would be infiltrating from the east and that I would be going in from the west, but we're switching sides. Make sure you're ready."

Klaus stood up and made to leave the room. He'd only been waiting for them to wake up.

Just as the girls began wondering about his unexpected thoughtfulness, he suddenly stopped in his tracks.

"And one other thing…"

He hesitated for a moment, which was unusual.

"…it's as you can see."

"What is?"

"I suppose that's not enough to understand, is it?" Klaus frowned disappointedly.

He went silent for a moment as though searching for the right words. "It can't have been easy, keeping up with a boss who couldn't teach or give proper instructions. Thank you."

And with that, Klaus briskly took his leave.

It took the girls a moment to register what had just happened. None of them so much as moved. It was only when they all glanced at one another and nodded that they could finally believe what they had just witnessed.

He had thanked them. That *aloof airhead of a man* had thanked *them*.

They didn't know why he'd said it. He might well have just done it on a whim.

Later, though, the girls would look back on that moment.

Later, they would realize that that was when they truly became a team.

The day had come to carry out their plan.

It was time to recover the bioweapon sample—an Impossible Mission that even Inferno had failed to complete.

The operation was scheduled for late on the night of the new moon, when the darkness would be deepest.

After finishing their final preparations, the girls snuck out of their respective hotels and raced through the darkness to the designated gathering point. There was a cliff overlooking the capital with a hill that provided a good vantage point, and that was where the team assembled.

That night, they weren't dressed in the student uniforms they used back in Din; neither were they wearing the tourist clothes they used to sneak into enemy nations.

No, they were clad in specialized black outfits designed for maneuverability and stealth. That way, they could utilize their full strength.

The laboratory they were going to infiltrate stood in the distance.

Seeing it reminded them just how difficult it was going to be to break in.

Its buildings were five stories tall. Only a small handful of authorized people were allowed on-site, and once evening came, they got kicked out, too. At night, the area was swarming with military guards. The only ways in were to sneak past the guards' watchful eyes and scale the compound's sixty-foot walls or to mount a bold frontal assault on the only road with access to the facility.

Inside lay the sample they needed to steal—the horrific viral weapon Abyss Doll.

The Lamplight members glared at the objective.

"The plan's still the same. We're infiltrating via two routes, with me taking one and the rest of you taking the other."

Klaus was wearing a suit, just like always, but in his case, the big change was to his hairstyle. Now his shoulder-length hair was tied back, leaving his forehead completely bare. That wasn't the hairdo of a man trying to blend into a crowd—that was a man ready for battle.

"The laboratory has both soldiers and spies stationed on-site. If anyone stands in your way, use deception to take them down."

The girls nodded.

With each sentence he spoke, their tension mounted.

The intelligence work they'd been doing had been nothing more than a prelude to this infiltration. It had had its dangers, but compared to the task on which they were about to embark, that preparation had basically been a walk in the park.

From there on out, a single wrong step could prove fatal.

"Let's go." Klaus raised his right hand up high. "And let's all make it out of this thing alive."

He snapped his fingers, and Lamplight melted into the darkness.

When the mission began, the girls started by forming a circle.

Then, the seven of them thrust their hands out and glared at one another.

Lily gave the opening shout.

"All right, time to decide who has to carry the bag!"

""""""Let's do this!""""""""

"Most common choice wins! Rock, paper, scissors—shoot!"

The girls all threw out "paper" in unison, with one exception—their white-haired sister, who had chosen "rock."

She instantly rushed at Lily and grabbed her by the collar.

"LILYYYYY! You said we were going to pick rock together!"

"Huh? Was *that* what I said?"

Whenever the group had to decide something, they always used that rock-paper-scissors variant to do so. Over time, it had devolved into a fierce, no-holds-barred information war.

Lily continued feigning innocence, and the white-haired girl was ultimately assigned the largest piece of luggage. Thanks to her loss, she was going to have to carry out the mission while wearing a massive backpack. Of all the girls, though, she was physically the strongest, so the delegation of labor ended up being fairly reasonable.

As the white-haired girl groaned at the rucksack's weight, the team set off.

Their first hurdle was the lighting that had been set up around the laboratory to deter intruders. The girls had to deftly weave their way between the lights in order to get close.

Then came the sixty-foot wall surrounding the compound.

"I don't know if it's a good idea to have all seven of us go up at once…"

On someone's suggestion, they sent their two most agile members up first to hang a wire near the top of the wall. As those two checked to make sure there weren't any lookouts up there, the next pair waited on standby halfway up. Once they made sure the coast was clear, they sent the last three up as well, including the heavily encumbered white-haired girl.

Although the wall was equipped with an alarm, they had laid the groundwork to make sure it would be disabled.

The seven of them then descended behind a large warehouse. The area was home to dozens of storage tanks several times taller than they were, as well as pipes going every which way, probably filled with gas or petroleum intended for use in the laboratory. The girls hid behind the tanks and each quietly readied her weapons.

They were deep in enemy territory now.

If anyone found them, they wouldn't be able to talk their way out of it.

From what they had heard, intruders were shot on sight.

"The next soldier patrolling this area has a key. We need to take it from him quickly," the black-haired girl whispered.

The others gulped. They hadn't been able to get their hands on the key ahead of time, so they had no choice but to secure it during the mission. Given the Empire's security, though, stealing it in advance would have taken a miracle.

Lily was torn between her knife and her automatic pistol, but she ended up going with the knife. She quietly applied poison to its blade.

She then noticed that her teammate beside her was sweating and barely breathing.

"Are you okay?" Lily asked as she rubbed her back.

"I'm pretty scared…" The brown-haired girl scrunched her face up in fear. "I have this bad feeling that won't go away. Like we're making a huge mistake…"

"Enough with that," the cerulean-haired girl sharply cut her off. "Now's not the time for doubts."

It was a prudent decision, but it had come a moment too late.

Lamplight had blindly accepted that everything was going to turn out all right, just because it was Klaus's plan they were following—but that belief was starting to waver. It was their first mission, and their elite boss's words were supposed to be their emotional bedrock.

They couldn't afford to doubt them. But no matter how hard they tried to believe, questions swirled through their minds all the same.

What if their foes were more powerful than Klaus expected?

What if their enemies had a plan even he had failed to anticipate?

Trying to retrieve the bioweapon had been enough to wipe out his old team, Inferno. Did they even really stand a chance?

The moment that fear was first born, it began spreading through their ranks like a virus.

"Don't you worry."

Before despair could swallow them up, though, Lily spoke. "If something goes wrong, we'll work together and make a plan—just like we always have."

Thanks to her speech, her comrades' fear subsided a bit.

Right when one of them was about to poke fun at Lily to further lighten the mood, they suddenly heard footsteps.

The soldier was coming, right on schedule.

The black-haired girl signaled the others with her eyes, and three of them dashed out from behind the tank. The guard was alone. They snuck up behind him, then pulled out a gag and shoved it in his mouth.

As he began panicking, another pair stepped forward to flank him. He was stronger than they were, but thanks to the joint-lock technique they employed, they were able to render him powerless.

Inside his pocket, they found the key.

The girls grinned.

"Now then, shall we interrogate him?" the black-haired girl asked with an air of grace while the others started lifting their captive. "Let's find somewhere safe to—"

A scream cut through the air. "Get back; it's dangerous!"

The girls reflexively leaped back from the body.

When they did, they felt a wind rush by them.

Someone had darted in too quickly for them to track visually and snatched the soldier away. This person hadn't made a sound and hadn't left a trace. The soldier's body had merely floated up, then vanished as though whisked away by a current.

Once they finally turned their gazes, they saw a tall man.

His arms and legs were lanky like a bug's, and the jacket he was wearing was navy blue. He had a sort of fickle energy to him that hardly seemed suited for the time or place. By the look of it, he was probably somewhere in his thirties, but the girls could just as easily have believed that he was still in his twenties. His bright hair came across as youthful, but his beard gave the impression of middle-age. All in all, his appearance almost came across as flippant.

The man tossed the soldier he'd just saved to the ground.

"That's weird. That idiot pupil of mine was supposed to come in from the west." An almost disappointed-looking smile crossed his face. "Did he change his mind at the last minute? Well, no biggie. I can just take you kids hostage, and that'll be that."

Lily knew that man.

She had heard his description from Klaus.

"Are you…?"

Her voice came out hoarse.

"…Mr. Guido?"

Guido was Klaus's mentor and a member of Inferno—a group that was supposed to have been annihilated.

By all rights, he shouldn't have been alive. And certainly not here in enemy territory.

"Huh?" Guido scratched the back of his head. "Why the hell do you know my name?"

"Teach told us about you once…"

"What, he was reminiscing? I guess that's fair. After all, it's not like I'm the only one whose information got leaked."

Guido's gaze slid across Lily's skin.

What did he mean by leaked information…?

Lily could feel her heart rate rise. Sweat broke out all across her body.

"Why did you know the routes we'd be taking…?"

"Bit slow on the uptake, aren't ya? I was with Inferno, and that means I used to live in Heat Haze Palace."

An ominous smirk spread across Guido's face.

"I've got that place bugged to the gills."

Upon hearing that, the girls finally understood everything.

Now they knew how the legendary spy team Inferno had been wiped out.

And how that tragedy had taken place in Klaus's absence.

It was because Klaus's mentor, Guido, had betrayed them.

At the same time, they also realized their peril.

If what they had heard from Klaus was true…

"So I've got your plan pretty much figured out. Welcome to your own personal slice of hell."

Guido pulled something spherical off his waist and threw it at them.

As Klaus raced through the facility, he heard an explosion off in the distance.

The sound had come from the west side of the laboratory—the side where the girls were making their approach. Someone must have found them, and a battle must have broken out.

The explosion's languid echo reverberated in his ear.

That sounds like the bombs my master used to use…

Explosions were just as varied as the bombs that made them. The distinction was slight, but Klaus could make it out.

What he was hearing reminded him of a certain man.

Although he didn't have any hard evidence yet, a memory flashed through his mind all the same.

When he'd found out about Inferno's demise, one corpse had given him pause.

It was his master's—Guido's.

They had located a body they assumed was his, but it was so badly mutilated, they couldn't be certain one way or the other.

As such, there was no way of knowing what fate had befallen Inferno's strongest combatant, the man whose skill exceeded even Klaus's— the man who could well and truly be called a monster.

Chapter 4

Lies and Retrieval

They were beside the laboratory's western storehouse, at the storage site for the facility's gas tanks.

The bomb Guido threw hadn't been particularly powerful; the surrounding tanks prevented him from using anything stronger.

Still, the force from the blast sent tingles across Lily's skin. She fled between the pipes, wincing all the while and eventually taking cover behind a water tank.

From there, she calmly analyzed the situation. Perhaps the bomb's true purpose had been to make noise. Guido must have wanted to let someone know a battle had broken out, though she didn't know who that could be.

The pipes running between the tanks extended out every which way like branches on trees—or even a forest of trees. As far as he could tell, the rest of the team had taken shelter among the plumbing as well.

Guido waited a little ways off from the tanks. He made no efforts to pursue them.

"What's the plan?" Lily heard the white-haired girl's brisk voice come from somewhere. "Guns and grenades are gonna be off the table if he follows us in here, right?"

The cerulean-haired girl haughtily replied. "No duh. We don't know how thick these tanks are. If they're full of gasoline or flammable gas, we could all go up in smoke."

"So we use knives, or we make a run for it. But..."

"Yeah, neither option seems great. I mean, he might look like a poser, but this is Teach's teacher we're talking about."

The one moment they had spent interacting with him had been enough for them all to realize just how skilled a spy their foe was. It was hard to envision a future in which they beat him, especially not in close-quarters combat.

Lily went silent, unsure of how best to respond.

She was good at bolstering the group's spirits—with or without evidence—but coming up with actual plans lay outside her area of expertise.

Then, she heard a calm voice coming from the other side of the water tank. It belonged to the red-haired girl.

"If we flee, he'll just run us down one by one. We'll have better chances fighting him together..."

Nobody disagreed.

They steeled themselves for a fight. If they tried to use the darkness to escape, there was a fair possibility that some of them would survive, but the odds that they would all make it were slim to none. Call it naive, but they had no intention of leaving anyone behind.

Guido could sense this.

"Seven on one, huh." He flashed them a strangely excited smile.

"You're goin' down one by one. Three minutes from now, I'll have you all on the ground."

Three minutes.

Lily had been afraid that they wouldn't last five, but she realized now that even that estimate had been generous.

Guido reached behind his back and drew a sword. It was an odd tool for a spy, but it seemed to be his weapon of choice nonetheless.

One of the girls audibly gulped.

Guido squared off, lowering his center of gravity.

There were forty feet between him and the gas tanks the girls were hiding behind. With his speed, he could close that gap in an instant.

For a few seconds, all was still.

Then, a whistle broke the silence.

The girls rushed from their hiding places in unison and fired off shots.

"Don't let him get close!" the black-haired girl shouted. "If he makes it to the pipes, our guns will be useless!"

All seven guns unloaded on him without mercy or hesitation. The girls knew that if they held back, they were the ones who'd end up dead.

Their barrage would have turned any normal person into Swiss cheese.

If only Guido were a normal person.

He zigzagged toward them, occasionally swatting bullets out of the air with his blade. He didn't look scared in the slightest. If anything, he was enjoying himself.

In what seemed like no time at all, he reached the area thick with piping, and the girls stopped shooting. Guns would do them no good now.

Instead, the seven of them sprang into action, laying wire traps around the pipes as they raced through the shadows. Luckily for them, the forest of tanks and pipes provided ample spots where they could hide.

Guido ignored the other girls and made straight for Lily.

She felt like a rabbit being chased by a lion. She ran atop the pipes as fast as her legs would carry her, but Guido was still faster.

He was going to catch her.

But right when that realization struck, she heard someone whistle.

That was the signal they used when setting traps.

Precisely two seconds after she heard it, Lily took a massive leap.

"Sorry!" Lily shouted. "But we've had plenty of practice being outmatched!"

All their training had given them a remarkable ability to rework plans on the fly and coordinate to make snap decisions.

As she somersaulted forward through the air, Lily shot a glance backward.

Guido was still holding his sword and coming after her, but he suddenly stopped in his tracks.

His right foot was caught in a tangled web of wires.

Someone must have laid a booby trap.

When Lily landed and looked up, she saw the cerulean-haired girl flipping Guido the bird.

With Guido rendered immobile, the other girls hurled knives at him, and their ash-pink-haired companion charged him from behind with a stun gun.

Thanks to their impeccable coordination, Guido was in serious trouble. With his leg trapped, there was no way he could dodge the knives hurtling toward him from every direction.

"What are you guys, dumb or somethin'?" he asked with a derisive laugh.

Lily stared in blank shock.

It happened in a flash.

All of a sudden, Guido's ensnared foot ripped through the wires holding it in place and slammed straight into the ash-pink-haired girl's gut; he evaded the knives with ease.

"Remember which country you learned about that trap in?"

He then swung his leg and dashed the ash-pink-haired girl against a gas tank. She let out a wordless moan, then crumpled to the ground.

"The Republic's tricks won't work on me," he said in a cool, level voice.

The young spy he'd kicked lay prone by his feet. She didn't get up.

"Six left."

The girls understood exactly what that meant.

Their pink-haired comrade, always the innocent, purehearted life of the party—Annette—was down for the count.

◇◇◇

The Galgad Empire had a number of covert operatives stationed at the Endy Laboratory.

Considering the bioweapon they had stored there, they would have preferred having more, but they'd made so many enemies around the globe that they lacked the spare personnel. Besides, guarding facilities wasn't exactly under their intelligence agency's purview. That was supposed to be the military's job.

As far as the Empire's spies were concerned, the Din Republic was already dead.

Not only had their one real threat, Inferno, been annihilated, but the Empire had also gotten its hands on a list of all the Republic's collaborators within their borders. The only thing left to worry about was

Inferno's sole survivor. That was why they had laid a trap for him at the laboratory and were waiting for him with waves of soldiers. Once he was out of the picture, the Republic was as good as theirs.

In the laboratory's admin building, one of the Empire's covert operatives—Eve—let out a yawn.

"Hey, are those Republic shmucks dead yet?"

Eve was a spy in her midtwenties. Her short brown hair gave her a young and girlish look, and her job centered around counterintelligence. Essentially, she was a member of the secret police tasked with tracking down enemy agents.

She was waiting in the communications room with a group of soldiers. Her nonchalant attitude earned her several frowns, but she just smiled and ignored them. Like in any country, the Empire's soldiers had a bit of a hard-on for order and discipline. Seeing her suck on her lollipop as she waited for news probably caused them no end of annoyance.

Still, they held their tongues.

The Empire's intelligence agency was completely independent of its Department of Defense, and as a consequence, there was no official hierarchy between the two institutions. Over time, though, the intelligence agency had unearthed a number of the army's scandals, and before they knew it, the spies could say "Jump!" and the military would have no choice but to ask "How high?"

A young male soldier promptly replied. "It appears that Bluebottle has engaged a spy or group of spies near the western storehouse. Another unit has also reported that they caught the trail of an infiltrator by the eastern gate. They're in the middle of tracking the intruder now."

"Heh. Then it's just like our intel said." Eve sat back down and planted her feet atop the desk.

The soldiers around her knit their brows in disapproval.

"Um...a question, if I may?" the young man asked.

"Hmm?"

"What chances do you think the Din Republic rats have of succeeding?"

"Hmm...," Eve replied. "None, I imagine."

"Surely it can't be that easy..."

Eve let out a derisive scoff. "The moment Guido…well, Bluebottle now, I suppose… The moment he betrayed them, we learned everything about all the Republic's spies. We know our enemy's techniques, their strengths, their weakness—even the plan they're using tonight."

"And that's going to be enough…?"

"See, Bluebottle planted bugs throughout his old home, and our foes have been living there completely blind to that fact. We know about every spy they sent to this compound, and they came here with bad intel, not even aware that we let them come." Eve snapped her fingers. "All we have to do now is swat a few loose flies."

Furthermore, they had installed traps and soldiers in every spot to which the Republic operatives were likely to flee. All that awaited them was ruin.

The young man didn't seem totally convinced. "But Mr. Bluebottle said there was a man we needed to watch out for."

"What, their boss? Nah, he won't be a problem, either. Bluebottle taught him everything he knows."

"Really…?"

"Apparently, they've sparred hundreds of times. But Bluebottle never lost once. As long as we leave him to Bluebottle, we'll be fine."

Everything she'd said had come straight from the horse's mouth. According to Bluebottle, he knew every aspect of their foe's fighting style, having raised him from early childhood.

"After all, we set up this plan to make sure we could kill him. They've been dancing in the palm of our hand this whole time. Now it's just a matter of time until we finish slaughtering them."

At last, the young man let out a deep sigh.

"It almost makes you feel bad for them."

"Hearing it all aloud…it does, doesn't it?"

Then, Eve happened upon an idea.

"Maybe I should put them out of their misery myself."

The soldiers flew into a panic. "Ma'am, you have orders to stay here."

"Excuse me? Don't you look at me like that. You think you can disobey me?"

"But…"

"*Well?*" Eve gave the soldiers a harsh glare.

The soldiers had gotten tired of this woman's smug superiority, and the young man took a resolute step forward.

"With all due respect, this laboratory is under the military's jurisdiction. If you need someone to fight the spies you lured in here, we're far more qualified to—"

However, he wasn't able to finish his sentence.

The thread wrapped around his thick neck snapped tight, and he let out a sad, frog-like croak.

The other end of the string was on Eve's fingertip.

She pulled it tighter, then sneered at the writhing soldier. "Sorry... What was that about fighting?"

Even though he had a much larger physique than her, his eyes were wide with fear.

She gave his head a kick.

"Listen, I don't care how much of a hotshot you are in the army; soldiers are a thing of the past. We don't need a bunch of apes who only know how to point a gun. With modern technology, war is simply too risky, too costly, and too wasteful. Am I making myself clear?"

That was why they needed spies. Anyone who could take over a country without jets or missiles was worth their weight in gold.

Eve kicked the man some more to drive her point home.

"You put so much work into training your body, and for what? You think your enemies are just going to walk up and fight you head-on? They'll shoot you from behind. They'll fight with deception, with poison. Without a decent mind to protect yourself, how do you plan on surviving in this new world?"

The moment the soldier looked like he was about to pass out, Eve let her string go slack.

"Now then, I have some spies to kill."

After catching his breath, the young man rushed to stop her.

"P-please, you have to wait! If the enemy is an elite spy, too, then you—"

"They can be whoever they please. I'm not about to get laid low by some surprise attack from the darkness. In my time with the secret police, dozens of enemy agents met their ends by my string." Eve flashed him her palm and the strings coiled around it. "I'll be sure to bring his head back for Bluebottle."

Just as she laughed, a message arrived in the communications room. The intruder had been spotted at the building that housed the main lab.

Perfect. Time to put him down.

As flippant as her attitude was, Eve was all business on the inside. She squeezed her gun tight, ready to act if she heard even the slightest sound. She advanced with hushed footsteps as she probed for signs of the enemy.

The lab's interior was cold and artificial. Its flooring was state-of-the-art linoleum—hygienic but not hard enough for footsteps to be too loud.

Eve silently let out her string to expand her web. The weapon was silent, of course, and thanks to the dim light, spotting it wouldn't be possible, either.

Now all she had to do was wait for the butterfly to drift into her spiderweb.

She felt a light twinge on one of her fingertips.

Got you... That's the weight of an adult man.

She reeled in her string and bound up her foe. Just as she thought, this guy was no big deal.

Eve chuckled to herself, then followed the threat so she could gun down her prey—

"*Gack.*"

A strange sound escaped her throat.

She didn't know when he had gotten there, but there was a man behind her.

He wiped the blood off his knife with an annoyed look on his face.

Eve didn't understand what had happened. Her throat felt warm, and when she reached up to touch it, a torrent of blood spilled from the slit.

"Just some nobody, then?" he murmured. His voice sounded almost listless.

Eve couldn't believe what she was seeing. Her web had caught someone—she was certain of it.

Now, though, her strings were in tatters, and the one being attacked was her.

"The Empire must really be shorthanded if these are the only operatives they can spare to guard this place."

The man caught Eve's body before she could hit the ground, then rummaged through her clothes. After determining she had nothing worth taking, he dumped her.

"I'm in a hurry. I don't have time to waste on the likes of you." He didn't even deliver the coup de grâce.

Instead, he raced off as though he'd lost interest, eventually vanishing from her sight altogether.

"Six left."

Guido's voice echoed coldly through the dark laboratory compound.

"Annette..."

What had once been a mere theory was now a certainty in Lily's mind.

It was all true. Guido's fighting skills were on par with Klaus's. He might even be stronger.

The way he had moved when overcoming their traps even resembled their teacher. There was no doubt he had once been Klaus's mentor.

As Lily hid, she felt like someone was squeezing down on her heart.

The man they were up against was on par with the one they'd fought for a month without securing a single victory. To make matters worse, they were already down a member.

Lily strained her eyes at the pink-haired girl Guido had struck.

She was lying on the ground, and her chest was rising and lowering ever so slightly. She was breathing.

"Thank goodness, she's still—"

"Killing is for amateurs."

Chains rattled as Guido dropped them by his feet.

After binding the pink-haired girl's arms and legs, Guido spoke again.

"You have ten seconds to get out of there. Each second beyond that, I break one of her fingers."

Lily gritted her teeth.

In the world of spies, taking hostages was fair game—in fact, everything was fair game.

To them, foul play was a way of life. If anything, his willingness to take a hostage was something to be praised.

With each passing moment, more sweat dripped down Lily's cheek.

She and her teammates exchanged glances as they stayed hidden in the shadows.

"Teach isn't here now..." Lily's gaze darted around. "Saving her is up to us. There's no other way."

She steeled her nerves.

Then, she slowly stepped out from behind the pipes and faced their menacing foe head-on.

Guido let out an impressed sigh. "Looks like someone made up her mind fast."

"Thanks for the compliment."

That was also the *only* nice thing he was saying about her, but better to not think too hard about that.

Behind her, she could hear the black-haired girl whispering.

"We have to come up with a plan while Lily buys us time."

Lily stretched her shoulders to feign composure.

So her job was to divert Guido's attention. She could roll with that.

"But you screwed up." Her foe didn't seem to be in any rush, either. "You shoulda ditched her and made a run for it. Once someone gets captured, it's their job to kill themselves as quickly as possible. You won't survive in this world long playin' buddy-buddy."

"Sorry, but the only thing we learned was that hostages are like injured swans."

"That damn kid. After all the work I put into teaching him properly..." Guido rubbed the back of his neck.

Lily clenched her fists and stared down her foe. "We made a promise that we'd all make it back alive."

Leaving a friend behind? That had never been an option.

"Without Teach and seven cuties like me, Lamplight wouldn't be Lamplight. I mean, a rainbow's got seven colors, and there are seven deadly sins… It's the perfect number. We've got Thea for lust, Sybilla for wrath, me for greed… Anyway, you get the idea."

The white-haired girl shot a retort from the darkness. "Who you calling wrath?!"

Even in their current predicament, her voice was as brisk and dignified as ever.

Cheered on by that fact, Lily's deflated expression softened a bit. "Six or eight just wouldn't be right. It has to be all seven of us going back with Teach."

"And I'm tellin' you that's naive."

The time for small talk was over. Guido switched his sword to a backhand grip and pointed its tip at his hostage. The bound, pink-haired Annette let out a weak moan.

"Bring it."

The implication behind his words was clear.

Drag this out any longer, and the girl dies.

"If you're as good as Klaus—"

Lily exchanged a glance with the other girls.

"—then I guess it's time for us to surpass him."

This was what they'd been doing for the past month.

A bunch of weaklings, working together to take down a Goliath.

In her heart, she knew—it was time to show the fruits of their labor.

They had never once succeeded, but they knew how it could be done.

"*…Use deception to take them down.*"

By piling lies on top of lies, it was possible to make someone mistake a zero for a one—or a one for a five. And that would give them an opening.

The red-haired girl walked up to Lily and quietly whispered the plan in her ear. Lily gave her a wink in lieu of a verbal confirmation.

Then, the battle commenced with one of the girls hurling a bomb at Guido.

A cloud of smoke billowed up. White fumes spread through the darkness, then faded.

Guido didn't move a muscle. He didn't so much as flinch. He just stayed by his hostage.

By the time the smoke screen cleared, the girls had already finished getting into position.

Two of them leaped out—the white-haired and cerulean-haired girls.

They were armed with gloves and a knife respectively, and they rushed at Guido from opposite sides. When it came to combat prowess, those two were the best in the group. Guido casually fended off their attacks with his blade, and the pair only barely managed to evade his counterattacks.

The white-haired girl had set her backpack down before diving into the fray. Newly unencumbered, she used her steel-plated gloves to block Guido's sword, and her cerulean-haired partner used the openings that created to level deft knife strikes at their foe.

However, Guido eventually put a stop to that, too.

His expression hadn't changed one bit during the entire skirmish, and he was even enjoying himself. Little by little, though, the girls found themselves completely on the defensive.

"Urk—"

When the white-haired girl groaned, her black-haired backup rushed in to lend them a hand with another smoke screen.

Smoke filled the air once more, and the white- and cerulean-haired girls used that opportunity to fall back.

They heard an annoyed murmur. "Enough of this shit."

Guido dashed away from his hostage. He had a new target—the black-haired girl.

She frantically tried to flee atop the pipes, but Guido wove through the snaking mess of metal without slowing down for a moment and quickly gained on her.

Suddenly, her foot slipped.

"Oh no…," she lamented as she toppled to the ground.

Down below, Guido was waiting for her with his sword at the ready. "You ain't getting away this time."

"Stay back…"

The black-haired girl choked the words out, her eyes dripping with tears. She scrambled pathetically backward with her butt still planted on the ground. The way she was twisting her body to the side and cowering accentuated her natural curves.

To make matters worse, her clothes caught on something while she was fleeing. They tore, leaving her buttocks fully bare.

The more she scooted backward, the more they ripped, and the more her seductive legs came into view.

"No… Don't come any closer…" Her voice came out frail and feminine, a far cry from her usual courageous tone.

"………"

Guido's response was as cold as ice.

"You've got the eyes of a vixen trying to lure in her prey. You tryin' to stir up my sadistic side or something?"

The girl immediately stopped her fake crying. "Maybe, but you're out of time."

A web of piano wires surrounded Guido and swooped toward him. He had already stumbled into their spiderweb of a trap.

Given his skills, he could cut himself free before they sliced him up, but—

"Magnificent."

—there was a follow-up ready for him, too.

Appearing from the dead of night, the man attacked from overhead, plunging a knife through the sole opening in the piano wire web.

That man was the one person Guido couldn't afford to ignore.

"This is checkmate for you, Guido—"

"You really think that's gonna work on me?"

But Guido didn't offer them the slightest opening.

Without so much as flinching at the fake Klaus's arrival, he sliced through the piano wire, coolly blocked the knife strike—which was miles slower than the real Klaus's would have been—and grabbed the imposter by the arm.

"Agh…" The girl let out a moan.

"The disguise ain't bad. Problem is, he always calls me Master." Guido hurled the fake Klaus with all his might.

As she flew through the air, her head skidded against the ground, and her mask came free. After rolling to a stop, she tried to lift herself up, but her arms quickly gave out.

The gentle red-haired girl who polished Lamplight's plans and strategies until they shone—Grete—was down for the count.

"Five left."

Guido tied up the red-haired disguise artist.

It only took him a scant few seconds. The black-haired girl didn't even have time to escape.

As she tried to scurry backward, Guido struck her jaw with the flat of his sword. The blow didn't look that hard, but she slumped to the ground all the same.

The beautiful, mature black-haired vixen who always brought the team together so elegantly—Thea—was down for the count.

"Four left."

At that point, the white- and cerulean-haired combatants finally caught up with him.

Guido evaded their attacks, then raced up a gas tank and looked around for his next prey.

Lily had been hiding and surveying the situation. Their eyes met.

"Y'know, your two buddies have been chasin' me around for a while."

He pointed his sword at her.

"You talked a pretty big game earlier—what've you been bringin' to the table?"

"………"

As Lily ran away, she cocked her head to the side.

As things stood, she was leaving planning, commanding, and fighting—pretty much everything—to the others.

"…Moral support?"

"Well, ain't that just peachy?"

Everyone had things they were good at and things they weren't. And that's just the way the world works.

As much as Lily wanted to defend her honor, though, she sadly didn't have time.

Guido had chosen her as his next target. He bolted toward her so fast, he seemed like lightning from the heavens.

There was no way she could dodge. His dropkick, so efficient it bordered on beautiful, smashed into her shoulder—

"That and *grit*!"

—and with willpower alone, she grabbed his leg.

Moral support wasn't the only thing she was good for. She had a weapon that was hers and hers alone.

The poisonous fumes, bursting from all over her body!

"Gas…?" Guido's eyes went wide for an instant. He quickly clamped his mouth shut.

"Do it!" she shouted, still holding his leg.

He immediately shook her off, but the damage was already done.

Guido staggered.

The team's two combat specialists launched what was now their third attack. "Fuckin' die already!" the white-haired girl cried briskly as she leaped, and her cerulean-haired cohort grinned haughtily as she thrust her knife at him.

The battle was over in an instant.

However, not in the way Lily had anticipated…

"Three left."

Struck on the chin by the flat of Guido's blade, the white-haired girl was the first to fall.

"Two left."

Then, after running afoul of his roundhouse kick, the cerulean-haired girl's body slammed into the piping.

The white-haired girl's—Sybilla's—cool, fearless remarks always pulled the team forward.

And arrogant as she was, the cerulean-haired girl's—Monika's—outstanding efforts had brought the team success after success.

Now they were both down for the count.

Screw this.

Lily broke into a run as well.

Two of her friends had just gotten pummeled before her eyes, and she was pissed. More importantly, though, she knew she couldn't afford to let this opportunity pass. Her toxin must have worked.

Guido shot Lily a look of admiration.

"So you're a little special, huh? You must be, if you can move around in this paralytic poison."

"Stops you; doesn't stop me!" she shouted confidently. She charged him, knife in hand.

However, he blocked the blow with ease. He was just as fast as ever.

"This can't be…" Lily gaped at him in shock. "Why didn't my poison work…?"

Her special gas had been sufficient to stop even Klaus for a short while.

How was Guido so unaffected?

"Nah, it worked. I quickly stopped breathing in, but still, this is some nasty stuff. Look, I can't even feel my fingertips."

Guido waved his hand, then clenched it to demonstrate.

"Still…you really think that's enough for you to beat me?"

Suddenly, Lily heard a voice from behind her.

"Miss Lily, run!" A teary-eyed girl rushed out on her own, then leaped at Guido from behind. "I'll buy you some time, so go—"

"Oh, shut up."

Before she could finish her sentence, she, too, fell victim to Guido's blade. His attack was so swift, she hadn't even been able to buy a couple seconds.

The team's timid, brown-haired worrywart, the one always acutely aware of the danger they were in—Sara—was tragically down for the count.

"One left."

Lily had to choose. Run or fight?

She hesitated for a moment—and that hesitation spelled her doom.

The instant she took a step forward, Guido was already there waiting for her.

He buried his fist deep in her gut.

"You're finished," he succinctly declared.

The girls had spent the past month constantly training.

And that training hadn't let them down. They had grown stronger, and their skills had advanced dramatically from where they had been before. The talent Klaus had seen in them had truly begun to bloom.

But at the end of the day, it had only been a month.

Guido had spent over two decades living as a spy on the front lines. He had never once neglected his training, and he had dozens of times more experience in live combat than the girls.

It was just math at this point. Nothing more, nothing less. They weren't ready to face him.

"Zero left."

The solemn verdict echoed in Lily's ears.
She crumpled to the ground.

Klaus was running.

The explosion he had heard earlier still weighed on his mind.

Impatience gnawed at him, and he raced through the laboratory as fast as he could.

He needed to hurry.

He wasn't going to lose an ally again.

He smashed a glass window with his foot, then leaped out of the building. He was on the third floor. He then cast out his wire, hooked it onto the adjacent building's roof, and smashed his way in through its window. He would have preferred moving about a bit more subtly, but given time was of the essence, shortcuts were in order.

How much longer would the girls be able to hold out against an elite spy?

No…if their opponent was *only* an elite spy, that would be one thing. *But if the person they're fighting really is* him…

…then he needed to act fast if he was going to save them.

Fearing the worst, he urged his legs on faster.

He soon found that the hallway in front of him was blocked by a large metal door. Klaus drew his picklock as he raced toward it. However, he discovered the door didn't contain any sort of keyhole.

A deep voice sounded out from behind him.

"That door isn't going to open no matter how skilled at lock picking you are. It's just a wall."

He turned to find a middle-aged man standing behind him. Klaus could tell by his outfit that the man was a seasoned spy, and he was accompanied by four soldiers to boot.

It would seem he had a new obstacle with which to contend.

Klaus tried to kick the door down, but it didn't so much as budge. The sensation in his foot told him that bit about it being a wall had been true.

The middle-aged operative spoke boastfully. "You want to take the shortest route to the gas tank repository, right? To save your little friends?"

"Oh? And how is it you know what I want?"

"A little bird told me all about you. Everything you people have done, you've done by our leave."

He burst into laughter, though it wasn't clear what exactly was so funny.

"The map your subordinates got their hands on was a fake. This here is a dead end."

"………"

"I can't believe you only just realized this was a trap. You're not too bright, are you?" The man shrugged disappointedly and let out another laugh. "It's pathetic, really."

His voice was downright grating.

"And you're supposed to be a teacher, too, aren't you? I have to tell you, those kids of yours are a hoot. Not realizing that the Empire was onto their every move, getting excited over the bad intel they got their hands on… I'll bet they had a blast playing spy."

"………"

"I mean, come on. From what I hear, they were a bunch of spy academy washouts. You seriously thought you could trick us by polishing a bunch of turds?"

"………"

"You should feel bad for being such a shitty leader."

The wall disguised as a door had no windows around it. It was well and truly a dead end.

The soldiers standing beside the middle-aged spy raised their submachine guns. It was the perfect weapon for firing down a straight, empty corridor.

The man raised his arm and coldly gave the order.

"Now, take your regrets to the—"

"I don't have time to mess around with you." Klaus had been hoping this fellow would spill useful information, but all he had gotten were unwarranted insults.

A large burst of flames rose up around his ambushers' feet.

The fire quickly filled the closed-off corridor, surrounding the men before they had a chance to flee. The only one unaffected by the blaze was Klaus, as he had backed up as far as possible and spread his flame-retardant suit out in front of him beforehand.

The flames died down just as quickly as they had arisen, but even that was enough to knock the soldiers out.

The middle-aged agent, who had used his allies as human shields, was the sole survivor. He screamed as the flames worked their way across his body, glaring at Klaus all the while.

"Y-you set a bomb...?"

"I fell for your trap on purpose." Klaus put his suit back on and took a deep breath. It was all almost anticlimactic.

The older man goggled at him in disbelief. "It doesn't make sense... How were you able to sense Eve's string? How did you know you were walking into a trap?"

"I just did. Although, there was also a bit of a trick to it."

"You little... You're nothing but a worthless spy from a worthless nation..."

The agent began backing off, but he soon stumbled and collapsed to the floor. His legs had suffered serious injuries as a consequence of the explosion.

"E-even if you get past me, you're still going to die anyway."

Spittle flew from his lips as he shouted.

"Bluebottle's going to massacre you. You—and all your pathetic little pipsqueaks!"

It was impressive, in a way, that he was still such a loudmouth after being bested so thoroughly.

However, Klaus had little admiration to spare for the man's ranting. "Enough with the wailing." Klaus drew a weapon as he closed the gap between them.

"No..."

"This isn't my favorite part of the job, you know. I'd rather you not annoy me while I have to do it."

The man's face went pale as a sheet.

What Klaus had produced was a thick, stained knife, jagged and nicked enough that cutting anything with it would be a slow, lengthy affair. It was a weapon designed for torture.

After laying Lily low, Guido let out an exasperated sigh.

Well, that was hardly satisfying. They barely even lasted a few minutes.

It was odd. Had the girls really believed they could beat him? They had gone up against Klaus for a month straight and come up short every time. What had possessed them to think they stood a chance against his mentor?

Guido threw a pair of handcuffs at each of the downed girls. When the restraints made contact, they snaked around his captives' limbs like living creatures and bound them up. The vanquished members of Lamplight probably wouldn't have been able to move anyway, but Guido wanted to be absolutely certain.

Right when he was about to throw a pair at Lily, his transceiver crackled.

"Bluebottle, what's the situation over there?"

The call was from one of his allies.

Annoyed by the unfamiliar code name, he spun the handcuff around his finger. "I'm just wrapping up. I've incapacitated most of the intruders, and I'm in the middle of securing them."

"Excellent work."

"Any sign of Klaus?"

"About five minutes ago, yes. One of our men located him in Building B, but it appears the target was able to escape. There's a good chance he threatened our man into spilling everything."

Guido's eyes went wide.

He had told them to report Klaus's movements in as much detail as possible, but his former student was making his way through the compound far faster than anticipated. The soldiers standing guard simply weren't able to keep up with him.

Seven more minutes till he makes it here... No, more like five.

Guido was confident he could take Klaus in a fight, but he also knew there was no poison half as deadly as overconfidence.

He was all too familiar with what Klaus was capable of.

"...Better make sure I tie these guys up on the double."

Guido hurled a pair of handcuffs at the last of his victims to seal the deal.

"Hyah!" She batted them away.

Guido looked over to find her glaring at him.

It was the silver-haired whelp—the one her allies called Lily.

"Scratch that... Looks like there's still one left," he said, restarting his countdown. "You're better off not resisting. Hurts like hell every time you move, I bet."

Guido had punctured her liver with great precision. Whenever the slightest pressure was applied to the wound, blood would pool in her liver, rapidly draining her stamina. Forcing herself to move in that state must have put a tremendous strain on her muscles.

"...Aren't you going to kill us?"

"Huh? No." Guido gave a small wave with his hand. "Don't worry, kid. I've got no plans of eliminating you right now, so you can go ahead and rest easy."

"All the more reason I can't rest, then."

And with that, Lily rose.

With shaky footsteps and a swaying torso, she tried desperately to straighten her knees and stand. She stumbled but made another attempt.

"Why even get up? It's not like you can beat me."

"I know what you're after..." Lily flashed him her pearly whites. "You're going after Teach, right? He's been your real target all along..."

"That he has."

Guido gave her a round of applause.

He wasn't mocking her—the praise was sincere.

"Got it in one. Dealing with him is just as important to the Empire as keeping the bioweapon."

Guido was under orders to do whatever it took to protect Abyss Doll. It was the ultimate deterrent, and as far as the Empire's politicians were concerned, their military capabilities were the backbone of their international influence. Even if war itself was an inefficient way of achieving their ends, that only made effective saber-rattling all the more valuable.

But in the Imperial intelligence agency's view, there existed a threat much more menacing that any bioweapon...

"Here's a fun fact for you. On the day Inferno got wiped out, the plan was to terminate him on his mission, too."

The fact that Klaus had been sent somewhere else that day hadn't been a mercy from Guido.

Klaus needed a very special trap if Guido wanted him dead. At worst, Klaus might even have ended up saving the rest of Inferno.

"But here he is, alive and kickin'. He even took out all the Imperial spies we sent to do him in. The way the Empire sees it, killing him is a top priority."

Their assassination attempt should have been enough to take out anyone, yet he had survived all the same.

No human could have pulled that off. Klaus referred to Guido as a monster, but in Guido's eyes, Klaus was something even more inhuman.

He was too big a threat to the Empire to be allowed to live.

"But this here's the end of the line. As his mentor, I can say with certainty that *not even Klaus* could survive this."

They had set everything up perfectly to ensure that.

Guido pointed his gun upward and fired. The shot echoed through the night sky—all the way to Klaus's ears.

"After hearing the gun and the bomb from earlier, he'll come here. And then, with his seven teammates taken hostage, he'll come after me. He'll know the odds are against him, he'll know it's pointless to fight me, but he'll put up a brave, gallant stand—and he'll die for it."

Lily laughed at Guido's explanation. "Ha-ha, you really think he'll come...? You sure he won't just leave us to our—?"

"That stupid pupil of mine will come."

He would.

As Klaus's mentor, that was the one thing of which Guido was certain.

"He won't abandon an ally. He'll sacrifice everything, walk into whatever trap he has to, but he won't leave a man behind. That's just the kind of person he is."

Even in this world of lies and deception, Klaus had principles he refused to break.

Given the choice between sacrificing the girls to survive and risking his life to save them, he would always pick the latter.

"Yeah, you're right. Ha-ha, no, no, I get it. He's totally gonna come." Lily exhaled and looked at the sky. "And when he does, he's gonna die protecting us."

"He cares too much about his allies. And that weakness makes it surprisingly easy to plan against him."

"Damn, you've really got us against a wall. If Teach comes, he's gonna die, and if he doesn't, then you'll kill us. We're doomed!"

A big grin spread across her face.

"Guess that makes it my job to stand up and fight you, huh?"

And so she did.

Her legs trembling, she struggled to her feet.

"If Teach is gonna die when he gets here, then I just have to take you down before he does."

"You know that's not happening, right?"

Guido lightly tossed a knife Lily's way.

She swatted it aside, but in doing so, she lost her balance and crumpled back onto the ground. Her legs were still weak.

"You can't win. You know you can't. So why do you keep getting up?" Guido scoffed.

He wasn't praising her blind, hopeless assault as a flight of youthful enthusiasm. The only thing in his voice was scorn.

"Because it feels nice here." The words spilled softly from Lily's mouth.

"...The hell?"

"That's why I'm working so hard."

Her tone became firmer.

"You probably wouldn't get it. You wouldn't get how much fun we had coming up with plans to take down Teach and bickering during our postmortems. You wouldn't get how every minute I spent with these girls fueled a fire inside me to be a better leader. You're a traitor; you could never understand." Lily rose to her feet and spat on the ground.

"What a pathetic person you are."

"........."

She was goading him.

He could see the contempt burning in her eyes.

However, Guido wasn't about to lose his cool over drivel like that. He had no obligation to lend an ear to the desperate grumblings of a spy who refused to accept when she'd lost.

"If anyone's pathetic, it's you." Guido laughed mockingly. "It feels nice? Yeah, I'll bet. Buncha washouts lickin' one another's wounds and getting to live in a swanky mansion? I bet you're having a blast. And I get why you'd want to protect that. But at the end of the day, all your buddy-buddy nonsense achieved was gettin' you taken hostage and weighing Klaus down."

It pissed him off that she still didn't get it.

It was precisely that softhearted comradery that had been their undoing.

He redrew his sword. "You're done."

With that, he smashed the flat of the blade into her gut. The attack was so fast she couldn't possibly defend herself.

Her back slammed into the pipes behind her, and blood trickled from her mouth.

"Take a good, long look. Look at what your posse of washouts was good for. And watch that stupid man die for the sake of his team."

"Gah…" Lily choked out a weak, hollow cry. "Teach, no… Stay away… He'll kill you…"

"He'll come, though. He will."

Unable to abandon his allies, Klaus was going to come despite knowing he couldn't win. The man, fatally unfit for spy work, was going to prioritize his subordinates' lives over the completion of his mission.

It had been about five minutes since Guido got his last call.

Where was he loitering while his helpless girls suffered?

Had he already arrived? Was he waiting for the right moment to strike?

"Hey, stupid pupil… Quit screwing around and get out here…"

If he was, he was leaving that poor girl to fight on her own.

"You're here somewhere, aren't you? C'mon… The enemy you're lookin' for is right in front of you, dammit!"

His voice burned with barely contained fury. He never knew the man he'd taken in, the man he'd raised, was such an idiot.

"The one who killed your family is right here!"

Guido shouted even louder, his voice booming through the night.

"The mentor you need to surpass is right here!"

He shouted again.

"Your student's ready to die if she has to!"

His voice echoed off the tanks—and that was it. No proud retort, no soft hints of someone sneaking around.

It didn't make sense.

Five minutes had come and gone, so…

"…Why isn't he here?"

"Mr. Guido, I have to ask…," Lily said quietly.

Guido looked down at her.

Then, a chill ran down his spine.

The girl's teary expression was gone, replaced by the cold, eerie gaze of a reaper come to herald his end.

He didn't get it.

If Klaus came, Klaus would die.

If Klaus didn't come, the girl would die.

The situation should have been utterly hopeless for her—

"…how much longer should I keep playing along with this game?"

—so why was she…smiling?

At that moment, he heard a message over his transceiver.

"Magnificent."

Guido would recognize that voice anywhere.

It had been transmitted from communications room one—the room right next to the main lab.

Instead of coming to Lamplight's aid, *Klaus was finishing his mission.*

It was the night before the mission.

After the end of their party, Klaus had called Lily to his room. She was blushing up a storm when she arrived; Klaus quickly realized she'd misunderstood but chose to save himself a headache by just ignoring it.

He cut to the chase. "I have a dangerous job I'd like to ask you to do."

A look of bewilderment crossed Lily's face. As usual, she made a few inane, self-aggrandizing remarks but ultimately ended up agreeing. "If it's for the team, then I'm in."

The genuine love she felt toward her teammates was liable to get her into danger, but it was also one of her most endearing character traits.

Klaus had high hopes for her. He lowered his voice. "In all likelihood, the Empire knows what we're up to."

"Huh?"

"*As I told you before*, all our conversations in Heat Haze Palace were bugged. They've probably been following our every move, and every bit of information Lamplight gathered was false intel prepared by our enemies. We may as well burn the lot of it now."

"Wait, but what about all our hard work?"

"It meant nothing."

"At least put it nicer!" Lily slumped her shoulders dejectedly.

The news came as quite a shock to her.

"I'm going to be blunt. A single month of cramming isn't going to be enough for amateur spies like you girls to surpass first-rate professionals. Especially not with my questionable teaching skills."

Lamplight had definitely grown. Given that they had started as all but dropouts, though, there was no way they would be able to go toe to toe with elite spies so quickly. It simply wasn't possible.

Lily cradled her head in her hands. "Great, *now* you start talking sense…"

"That's fine, though. We're going to feign ignorance and go ahead with the infiltration anyway."

"But how're we supposed to get the bioweapon like that?"

"Because they'll think we know nothing, our foes will underestimate me and try to lure me into traps. That knowledge will let me counter them. I'll turn the tables on the people they send after me and steal intel from them directly."

"Sounds like it's gonna be superhard for you…" She wasn't wrong, but it was the best option they had.

Fortunately, he had spent the last month with a group of girls trying to catch him in traps, so he was certainly warmed up for the task.

"Meanwhile, there's someone I want you to deceive."

"So we're gonna be a diversion?"

"Exactly. Your true mission is to feign weakness—and to use that to create an opening."

That was the real reason he had gathered the girls together and why he had trained them.

If *he* really had betrayed them, then Klaus wouldn't be able to pull this off on his own.

Upon hearing the full scope of their plan, Lily pressed a finger against her cheek and tilted her head to the side.

"Hmm… I'm not totally sure I followed all that, buuut…"

Always with the theatrics, that one.

"…basically, our job is to take on this Imperial spy who's been laughing at us from the shadows this whole time, then use all our lies and training and comradery to land a big ol' wallop right in his face and be like *Ha, serves you right*?"

The corner of her lip curled upward.

"I gotta say… I think it's gonna feel real darn good."

However, that shameless mental fortitude of hers was precisely why Klaus knew he could count on her.

He spoke, his tone earnest and firm.

"Show him what you learned from our game of cat and mouse—and use deception to take him down."

"Can you hear me, Master? It's certainly been a while."

His pupil came through loud and clear.

Guido looked at the light on his transceiver to double-check where the call was coming from.

Communications room one…?

That was right next to where the bioweapon was stored at the southern-most end of the facility. Guido wasn't anywhere near it, so Klaus must have had his run of the place.

"I'm calling to report that I just secured the bioweapon."

Klaus spoke in the same disaffected voice Guido remembered. Of course he had the bioweapon; it had been obvious from the moment the call came in.

No, the problem was that he had gone to the main lab instead of saving the girls in the first place.

"Never thought you'd prioritize your mission over rescuin' your team," Guido replied candidly. "Gotta say, that one's a shocker."

Klaus should have come after him right away.

This was an unexpected turn of events—but it was still one for which he had an answer.

"You have five minutes to get your ass over here before I start killing the girls one by one."

His students' lives were still in his hands. Nothing had fundamentally changed.

Klaus would come. And Klaus would die.

"No...," Klaus said. *"...I won't be coming."*

"What?" Guido was sure he'd misheard.

A dumbfounded murmur escaped his lips.

Klaus then explained himself, deadpan as ever.

"I completed the mission, so I'm heading home. Even if I came, I know I can't beat you in a fight. I have my own survival to consider."

And that was that, as if this were a casual conversation.

"You set quite an impressive stage—my pupils in danger, my foe a traitor, and my master secretly being alive—but sadly, you and I won't be fighting today."

"...What are you talking about?"

"You failed to protect the bioweapon, and you failed to kill me. There really isn't any more to it."

Any normal spy would have agreed that this was the correct decision. Sacrificing his allies to complete his mission was the rational thing to do.

But that was a choice the man Guido was talking to would never be able to make.

Klaus would never abandon a teammate. That was the whole premise behind the plan.

"Don't make me say it again. You have five minutes to make it to the west side of the compound. If you're not here, I'll kill them."

"Don't make me say it again. I'm not coming."

"You're just going to abandon these girls—your allies?"

"That's the plan."

"You know the Empire's gonna torture 'em, right?"

"I hear gut punches are just the thing."

It was downright uncanny.

How could he be so calm about all this?

Why did he sound so in control when his teammates' lives were in imminent danger?

Cold sweat trickled down Guido's back.

Guido's men had listened to all the conversations in Heat Haze Palace, and on the fourth day after the girls moved in, Klaus had sworn that he wouldn't let them die. Had that promise been a lie? Had he been playing them for fools and sending them to their deaths?

No. This man was incapable of something like that.

As someone who knew Klaus better than anyone, Guido could say that with confidence.

"But, Master, you're operating under one giant misapprehension."

"Hmm?"

As confusion racked Guido's brain, Klaus's words sank into it like water into parched soil.

"I had a feeling from the start that someone from Inferno turned traitor. I am surprised it turned out to be you, but I knew all along that Inferno's destruction was an inside job."

"You didn't have any proof, though. How could you be so sure?"

"I just was."

"…Y'know, sometimes I forget how much of an airhead you are."

"If I absolutely had to give a reason, I probably figured it out when I found the bugs you planted. And besides, it was hard to imagine a group as strong as ours getting wiped out by anything but treachery from within."

He found the bugs?

But wait, that meant…

"As such, everything we did was with the knowledge that a traitor was wiretapping us."

"Everything…?"

"*For example, one of our rules was to never use our special abilities inside Heat Haze Palace.*"

Suddenly, Guido remembered.

According to his men who'd been in charge of the wiretap, the girls had reacted with confusion when they first arrived at the manor.

The odd passage, *Rule ㉗: Give it your all when you're out and about*, hadn't made any sense to them.

"*You didn't know that one of the girls was a poison user, did you?*"

"………"

"*No, you didn't. You thought you knew what the girls were capable of, but in truth, you knew nothing. Not even you could have known about the hidden geniuses lurking in the spy academies.*"

Klaus raised his voice until he was practically shouting.

It was like he wanted to declare his superiority as loudly as possible.

"*What I'm saying is: There's no need for me to come. The girls will beat you all on their own.*"

"They'll what?"

"*Each and every one of them is an even greater prodigy than me. You couldn't possibly prevail against them.*"

Guido couldn't even begin to understand what Klaus was saying.

Klaus was going to abandon the girls, and they were going to beat him themselves.

The plan was completely detached from reality. It was little more than a delusion.

That was when he saw Lily and the confident smile stretching across her face.

"Ha-ha, guess that means I can stop stalling now."

"Stalling…?"

"Now, I'm gonna get seriouser than serious. You'll finally get to see what happens when Lily, Din's slumbering wunderkind, finally wakes up."

Was she trying to imply that she had been holding back this whole time?

Even after having been knocked down countless times already, she rose to her feet once more.

Guido couldn't begin to fathom the source of that tenacity of hers.

"...Hidden geniuses? What a joke. The only reason I don't know who you people are is 'cause you're a bunch of washouts, right? I made sure to keep tabs on all the top students."

"Th-that's not true..."

It clearly was.

Klaus must have just been lying. There was no way in hell there could be seven bigger monsters than him.

Still, I don't get it. These girls can't beat me...so ain't that stupid pupil of mine coming?

Was he really beating a tactical retreat? No, he must have some sort of plan.

Did he really think that a little out-of-the-box thinking would be enough to beat Guido?

"Comms room two." Guido made another call. "Did Klaus's transmission really come from comms room one?"

"It did. He knocked out the soldiers stationed there and was occupying the room. We ran over, but there are signs he left."

The spy stationed in the other communications room explained the situation.

"Klaus is...nowhere near you."

"This doesn't add up..."

Help wasn't coming, and Guido was sufficiently stronger than the girls that they wouldn't be able to pull any cheap tricks on him.

That left two possibilities.

One—that Lily truly was a secret weapon of the Din Republic who had somehow escaped Guido's notice.

Or two—that Klaus really was abandoning them.

The former simply wasn't true. Guido could tell that much from fighting her. She certainly had *some* skill, but it wasn't polished in the slightest.

So was it the latter? He loved his allies so dearly and went to such lengths to protect them; was he even capable of that?

"Did my stupid pupil...actually change...? Is he really not gonna come help his—?"

"I'm telling you: We don't need any help." Lily cut him off.

She gave him a cold smile.

"How much longer are you gonna stand there thinking of me as a little damsel in distress who needs saving? I'm no damsel—I'm cheeky, I'm strong, I'm cool, I'm pretty, and I'm the leader of this here team."

She stood on her own two legs, gallant and brave.

"See, there's something I found here in Lamplight. I found a way even a washout like me can blossom. And so as its leader, it's my job to take the whole team's skills and power and pound them into you!"

Her voice was unwavering.

Despite having her back up against a wall, her eyes burned with fierce determination.

"You talk a big game for a washout."

"Yeah, keep looking down on me. See how that ends for you."

Lily spread her arms out wide.

"I'm code name Flower Garden—and it's time to bloom out of control."

She introduced herself boldly enough that it called her instincts as a spy into question.

The change was immediate—something began bubbling across her body.

Just like flowers coming into bloom.

"Foam...?" Guido growled.

Lily's skin had just released a massive amount of bubbly foam.

It poured out from her sleeves, her collar, her buttonholes, and her skirt.

After gushing forth from every conceivable opening in her clothes, the soapy bubbles spilled out onto the ground around her. Even after landing, though, they refused to pop, instead flowing around and sticking to the pipes and tanks.

The bubbles were a shade of purple so noxious that just looking at them would have been enough to make anyone want to give them a wide berth.

As they spread, they let out a horrible burbling noise.

In the blink of an eye, the entire area was bathed in her foam.

"Y'see, Teach was able to beat my poison gas, too."

"Huh?"

"So after a month of effort, this is the innovation I landed on. A poison foam that makes full use of my special trait."

Guido had experienced firsthand what that was.

The girl had been able to move freely amid a cloud of powerful paralytic gas.

If he hadn't acted fast, he would have been in danger from such a powerful toxin, yet she had shrugged it off like it was nothing.

In short, the girl was immune to poison.

Lily stuck her tongue out at him. "Wanna find out how strong this stuff is?"

The only way her tone could have been more carefree was if she were literally humming.

Was the foam really poisonous, then?

Guido fell back as he observed the ever-expanding mass of bubbles.

Some of what she said was probably a bluff...

He calmly analyzed the situation.

There was no good reason for her to go and reveal her ability like that.

...but what if the poison's strong enough that it'll kill me in a single hit?

That wasn't fear talking. As a spy, he had to consider every possibility.

As Lily stood in the unidentified froth, she gave him a provocative smile.

She didn't look afraid in the slightest.

She knew how much stronger he was and that Klaus wasn't coming to help, yet she was proudly baring her teeth.

Could it be true? Could it be that she wasn't a washout, but a genius?

Could any person truly act so composed in a situation they knew was hopeless?

Questions swirled through Guido's head, and an instant later, he made his choice.

"Hey, stupid pupil, you still there?"

"Yes?"

"You probably can't see, but the only girl still able to fight is Lily."

"That's more than enough."

Klaus's voice was brimming with confidence.

I just don't know...

In that moment, Guido began worrying for the first time.

It stings, but he's right… I don't know how strong the girl's tolerance is…

If she were any other spy, he'd have been fine.

He had memorized everything about all the Din Republic's official spies—as well as all the top students at the spy academies. Even beyond that, word about the male problem students often got back to him, too. He could have easily come up with strategies to deal with any of them.

This was his sole blind spot—underachieving female students.

"No, this is fine… Whatever her plan is, I'll just smash through it head-on."

He had fought his way out of plenty of grim situations when he didn't have a lot of intel with which to work.

He relaxed his body and waited for Lily to approach.

All he had to do was take her hostage and force Klaus to come. That was all there was to it.

She seemed to be ready, too. Clad in the foam—

—she dashed toward him.

She ran with all her might.

Her speed wasn't anything to write home about, but her intensity set Guido's nerves on edge.

She closed in on him, still wearing her eerie lather like armor.

Her long hair disheveled and a roar coming from her throat, she charged into him head-on—

"Wha—?"

—then let out an abrupt cry.

"Too slow."

The conclusion Guido arrived at was that he simply had to attack fast enough that she couldn't pull anything.

Lily didn't seem to realize he had stepped toward her. She hadn't even seen him. Guido had intentionally staggered his advance to make her misconstrue the distance between them.

He didn't give her so much as a chance to react.

After carefully avoiding her foam as he passed her by, he landed a clean blow on her back with his sword.

"Gah!"

She had finally reached her limit. Guido could feel the power drain from her body.

The silver-haired novice whose resolve and shamelessness were a match for any elite spy's—Lily—was down for the count.

"Zero left."

With that, he had bested them all.

Guido was certain he had ruined their plan. He wiped his sword clean and sheathed it.

As he did, he suddenly noticed the foam bubble that had landed on the back of his hand. Apparently, he hadn't been able to dodge them all.

He reflexively swatted it off, but his skin was the same as ever. The suds hadn't caused any rashes or pain. As far as he could tell, it was just regular old foam.

"...Was the part about the poison a lie? Or is it just slow-acting?"

Either way, it didn't seem to be deadly.

Exasperated, he looked around at the seven girls sprawled out on the ground.

Even just a glance was enough for him to notice that they all had different hair colors—ash pink, red, black, white, cerulean, brown, and silver. Lily had likened them to a rainbow, and sure enough, there it was. Seven colors.

As he looked at the defeated spies, Guido's mouth curled into a grin.

"Klaus, all your girls are—"

However, he didn't get a chance to finish.

All of a sudden, something came rushing down at him from overhead.

"Wha—?"

One of the pipes was falling toward him.

The impacts from the fight must have knocked one of its bolts loose. Guido immediately leaped backward.

Had Lily used her foam to lure him there?

The timing seemed too good to be true, but the logical part of his brain quickly took over.

That wasn't it. The accident must have been just that—an accident.

It was probably random, he thought. Merely a weird coincidence.

After all, there was something he didn't know.

Guido was *wholly unaware of a girl who could predict accidents.*

And even if it was on purpose, a measly pipe is hardly gonna be enough to—

A falling pipe was something he could handle with ease. In fact, he was already clear of the impact site.

Then, something moved.

In Guido's peripheral vision, he saw something shift in the sea of foam Lily had laid.

However, he couldn't react. He was already leaping backward, so he had no way of dodging.

The thing raced toward his back, and pain shot through him.

"Agh?!"

Blood gushed from his mouth, and he felt a burning sensation in his back.

But Lily was still down. The other six shouldn't have been able to move, either.

What was going on?

Guido fought through the pain to look behind him.

There, he saw the unsheathed blade that had appeared out of nowhere *from the foam he had assumed was poisonous...*

"How unlucky..."

...as well as a blond girl.

She was holding the knife tight and stabbing it into his back.

His assailant, who possessed a certain doll-like beauty, turned her melancholic gaze toward him.

"Our first coordinated plan, and I get stuck with the hardest job..."

What Guido was seeing was impossible.

He took another dumbfounded look around.

There were seven girls lying prostrate on the ground in the laboratory's western storehouse. He had counted right the first time.

In short, the only possibility was—

"An eighth...?"

The one with white hair had been carrying a massive backpack—was that where she'd been hidden? Afterward, she must have used Lily's foam as cover to get into position.

Even if he understood it rationally, he still couldn't come to terms with it.

At Heat Haze Palace, hadn't Klaus always called them *you seven*? Hadn't the girls always said *"the seven of us"*? Didn't Lily just finish proudly declaring that there were seven colors in a rainbow?

There were supposed to be seven of them.

All of a sudden, he got another call from communications room one.

"By the way, I didn't mention it..."

A cold voice echoed through his transceiver.

"...but one of our rules was that the eight of you have to live your lives as seven people."

"What...?"

"I'm sure you've figured it all out by now, so as a special favor, allow me to introduce the team to you.

"Our boisterous first member has silver hair, a loud mouth, and a penchant for making trouble—Lily.

"Our no-nonsense second member has white hair, gets along well with Lily, has a foul mouth, and is always the first into the fray—Sybilla.

"Our timid third member has brown hair, a good head on her shoulders, and a nervous temperament—Sara.

"Our graceful fourth member has black hair, a knack for seduction, and is the team's de facto leader—Thea.

"Our demure fifth member has red hair, a tactical mind, a ladylike tone, and a bad habit of calling me Boss—Grete.

"Our arrogant sixth member has cerulean hair, a tomboyish tone, and the skills to back her attitude up—Monika.

"Our purehearted seventh member has ash-pink hair, an irreverent manner, a simple spirit, and she always helps keep the team's morale up—Annette.

"And our quiet eighth member has blond hair, showed up late to the group after running into a series of accidents, and mostly kept to herself at first—Erna.

"I may have called them you seven, *but there are eight girls in all."*

The trick had been built around the wiretap.

If Guido had seen them with his own two eyes, it would have been obvious in an instant that there were eight of them, but distinguishing between eight girls by just their voices was no easy feat.

"Just how deep...did the lying go...?"

Klaus's first meeting with the team had been a lie, the oath he swore to them was a lie, their games of cat and mouse had been a lie, their daily lives had been a lie, Lily's posturing had been a lie, and her poison foam had been a lie—all to mask that single attack.

Guido finally realized the truth.

The girls had never harbored any illusions about being able to beat him.

They had traded a month of their lives, just to land a single blow.

However, that realization came too late.

A spurt of blood gushed from his back.

As she watched Guido collapse, Lily squeezed her fists tight.

Elation filled every inch of her body.

It worked...!

That was the grand trap Klaus had set—having the eight girls live as though there were only seven of them.

Heat Haze Palace Communal Living Rule ㉖: Work as seven to live together.

When the girls first read the rule, they didn't understand why it was there. After all, when Lily arrived and when Klaus first appeared, there actually *were* only seven of them. The rule came across as childish.

But on the second evening, it all became clear.

That was when Erna, who had been delayed by a series of vehicular mishaps, finally showed up.

The eight of them were being told to work *as seven*.

As such, at least one of them made sure not to talk whenever all eight of them were together.

Also, they did their absolute best to avoid calling one another by name.

Selling the lie had taken a coordinated effort by the entire team. Together, they had set a trap and used their foes' bugs against them.

Of course, we still only barely pulled it off...

Lily chuckled to herself, then got back to work.

Erna reached into Guido's pocket and pulled out a key.

Lily took it from her, then began releasing the girls Guido had tied up. None of them were seriously injured. That came as a big relief, but more than anything, she was again impressed at the precision of Guido's technique. For a spy, being able to hurt a foe without leaving any wounds or injuries was an invaluable skill—especially when trying to threaten them into giving up information.

"C'mon, let's get out of here! Teach can handle the rest!"

As Lily scurried around freeing the others, Erna gave her a disappointed look.

"So much for that attitude from earlier..."

"Oh yeah, no, we're all damsels in distress, and we definitely need saving!"

"Why would he make a whole team of damsels in distress?!"

If they ran into a traitor from Inferno, the girls' job was just to keep them busy. Meanwhile, Klaus would handle everything related to actually securing the bioweapon. All grandstanding and posturing aside, the thing Lily wanted most was to get as far away from this terrifying place as possible.

After quickly freeing all the others, Lily finally reached her white-haired teammate. Then, right as she got the brilliant idea of doodling on her face—

"Behind you!"

—she heard Erna scream.

Lily was able to dodge the sword flying at her head, but only by the slimmest of margins. One of her hair ribbons was shredded to pieces.

Erna's sensitivity to danger was really something else. Developing it must have taken a truly unfortunate life indeed.

In any case, though, Lily really wished she wasn't seeing what she was seeing.

Guido got to his feet. He was breathing hard, and his eyes had a feral gleam to them.

"I stabbed you, though, I'm sure of it..."

"Yeah, but I shifted to catch the blow between a muscle and a bone."

He wiped away the blood trickling from his mouth. "Still passed out for a bit, though. Gotta admit, it's been a while since the last time that happened."

Erna bit her lip as she stood by Lily's side. However, nobody could possibly blame her for what had happened. Seeing through an elite spy's trickery was far easier said than done.

"This guy's seriously a monster..."

Guido combed back his hair with his hand, leaving a rusty streak thanks to the blood. He stared the girls down as the wind gradually dried his newly blood-caked hairdo.

"Ruuun!" On Lily's signal, Lamplight fled.

Her reasoning was simple: Guido was seriously wounded, so there was no way he'd be able to give chase.

He was acting tough, sure, but it had to just be an act. And her reasoning was dead wrong.

"Ah—"

Guido's speed didn't seem to have suffered in the slightest.

By the time they saw him leap, he was already springing from pipe to pipe, almost dashing through the air. It was no more than a blink of an eye before he was directly over the fleeing girls' heads. He launched something at them.

Blood.

With a big swing of his right arm, he hurled a handful of blood at them like a shotgun blast. The fluid was so sticky, they couldn't get it out of their eyes, and it slowed them down just the way he wanted.

His target was Lily, and his kick whizzed through the air and made straight for her face. At the last moment, the white-haired spy blocked the blow. However, his foot continued on unabated, sending Sybilla crashing into Lily. They both went flying and slammed into the two girls behind them. They all tumbled to the ground.

One kick had laid four of them low.

They were no match for him.

Guido was a wounded beast now.

The girls were utterly helpless.

"A tenth of a second." Guido raised a finger. "That's how much you slowed me down. Congratulations."

That was little more than a rounding error.

They had thrown every scheme they had at him, and that was all it had accomplished.

Guido looked down at the still-prone spies and pointed his gun at them. He wasn't worried about the gas tanks behind them. He knew he wouldn't miss.

All the emotion left Guido's expression as he placed his finger on the trigger.

"Magnificent."

A cold, imposing voice rang out.

Guido's gun was knocked aside. He leaped away from the girls, just as Klaus landed on the very spot he'd been standing.

"Teach!" Lily joyfully cried.

Klaus turned to her and tossed her his briefcase. "This is the bio-weapon. Take it and run."

"Wow, you really got it all on your own…"

"Only because you ladies distracted my master."

Klaus turned away from his team and looked at Guido.

"Go on ahead; I might be a while. Use route number four to get back home. And like a fountain welling up from a plateau, remember your training."

"That doesn't make any sense, but you got it." Lily went to check on the others.

Behind her, Klaus and Guido were having their reunion.

"It's been a while, Master."

"Klaus…"

Lily was extremely curious—what would this mentor and pupil have to say to each other when one of them should have died?—but now was no time for voyeurism.

The girls made a beeline toward the facility's perimeter.

"My subordinates did some fantastic work, I see." Behind them, they heard Klaus's voice. "Your movements are a tenth of a second slower."

It rang with confidence.

"Looks like I finally caught up."

Filled with rage, Guido bellowed in reply, "KLAUS!"

As she fled, Lily looked back over her shoulder.

Guido was charging at Klaus, gun at the ready. He was moving fast enough that she knew she wouldn't have been able to react.

"I'm sorry, Master..." Klaus's lips moved ever so slightly. "...but as you are now, you aren't qualified to be my enemy."

The last thing Lily saw was Guido spinning spread eagle through the air.

She couldn't tell what Klaus had done.

The two of them were on a whole different level, and their battle had been too fast for her to follow.

However, it was clear that Klaus had emerged the victor.

Five minutes later, the girls reached the laboratory's wall and made their escape through a rain of gunfire.

Then, after losing their pursuers, they headed to a predesignated truck and made their way across the border hidden among its cargo.

And with that, their Impossible Mission ended in success.

Epilogue

Loss and Rebirth

A week had passed since the completion of the mission.

The Lamplight girls were gathered in the main hall, and all were carrying suitcases. A couple of them were restlessly checking the contents of their bags, and several of the others were yawning sleepily. They had been up late partying, so none of them was exactly well rested. There were also some members of the team who hadn't managed to finish packing yet.

Chief among that group was Lily. She had tried to cram all her clothes in her bag, then started dragging everything out again once she realized there was no way in hell it would fit. She'd loaded in too many nonessentials. Upon retrieving the pistol she had haphazardly stuffed inside, a pleased grin spread across her face.

"Man, when I look at my spy tools, it brings me right back to when I played Guido for a fool... And in that moment, Lily the Great Pretender was born."

The white-haired girl, who had long since finished her packing, offered a brisk rebuttal.

"I dunno, sounded to me like you were talking out of your ass back there. I mean, divvying up the seven deadly sins?"

"Nobody asked you, Wrath."

"Just to ask before I clock you, which sin are you?"

"Oh, I'm greed. And envy. And gluttony. And sloth. And pride."

"Wait, you're not even divvying them up!"

Back when they listened to Lily's conversation with Guido, all the girls had silently thought the same thing.

Tricking Guido might have been part of their plan, but Lily had been spouting off some pretty random nonsense.

At the end of the day, though, it had worked, so it was hard to blame her for reveling in the victory.

However, one member of the group poured cold water on her enthusiasm.

"And besides...," Erna said. "We barely even did anything..."

"Wh-what are you talking about?!"

Erna took a seat atop her suitcase, which was almost as tall as her, and idly kicked at the air. "All we did was sneak into a corner of the laboratory, get in a single hit on a single enemy, and then run away..."

"Yeah! Pretty impressive, right?"

"And in the same time, Teach knocked out a dozen guards, disguised himself as a soldier, snuck in, snatched a key, opened three safes, blackmailed a researcher, stole the bioweapon, destroyed their research results, killed four enemy spies, and also took down the enemy who we could barely touch."

"......................................"

Lily took a good long while to mull over the stark truth with which she'd just been presented. She then opened her eyes wide, strode right over to Erna—

"Take that! Cheek pokes!"

"Hwuh?"

—and offered a carefully considered counterargument.

"Divine punishment for being a buzzkill!"

"Sh-shtooop!"

"Oh wow, your skin is so soft. I guess you really *do* exist."

"Of coursh I do!"

"It's just—your presence felt so faint during the mission, it was like... did she dissolve into thin air or something?"

"You're horrible!"

Lily prodded both of Erna's cheeks simultaneously as though to make sure she hadn't turned incorporeal in the last two seconds.

As she kept going, Erna's expression grew more and more pained, eventually causing the rest of Lamplight to leap at Lily. "Quit bullying her!"

Lily responded by obstinately continuing to poke Erna's cheeks, while the others tried to pry her off. As Erna was shaken back and forth, she let out an alarmed cry.

"Y-you really should be careful around me, or—"

"Ah! The floor!"

Lily's foot slipped.

She had tripped over a bump in the carpet, and when she fell, she took the rest down with her. The latch on the suitcase Erna had been sitting on came undone, and its contents poured out all over the main hall. "How unlucky…," Erna moaned.

Lily lay faceup with the other girls pinned beneath her.

Instead of listening to their demands that she get off them, though, she instead just gazed at the ceiling.

"Ahhh…"

Her voice sounded almost like a sigh.

"Guess we're not gonna be able to hang out like this anymore, huh."

That was why the girls had packed—they were going their separate ways.

"That's right."

They heard a calm voice.

Klaus was sitting on a sofa over in the corner. "Lamplight was a provisional team designed to take on a single Impossible Mission. With the mission complete, the team's being disbanded. You did well."

The girls responded with slight nods.

The only reason they had been assembled was as a countermeasure against the traitor from Inferno. Now that they had fulfilled their roles, they were to disperse. There was no good reason to continue putting a bunch of inexperienced girls through these harsh missions.

The plan was to have them return to their respective spy academies. The next time they did fieldwork, it wouldn't be after a provisional graduation but after they had succeeded in graduating the old-fashioned way.

"Now then, it's about time." Klaus knew when the train was coming.

They had already finished saying their good-byes the night prior, so the girls made their final preparations, then headed to the front entrance with their suitcases in tow.

One by one, they each thanked Klaus for everything as they left.

Klaus wordlessly saw them off.

"........"

"Hmm? What is it?"

The last to leave, Lily, took an interest in his expression. His lip had twitched for a moment, like there was something he wanted to say.

"No, it's nothing." He shook his head. "I hope we meet again someday."

"Yeah. It probably won't be for years to come, but..."

Lily gave him a small smile.

"...see you again someday."

After watching the girls go, Klaus got to work on Lamplight's final duty.

His destination was the Din Republic's Cabinet Office Building. It was an unremarkable edifice in the heart of Din's capital, about two hours' drive from Heat Haze Palace. After making sure he wasn't being followed, Klaus headed into the Foreign Intelligence office.

An older man with gray hair was waiting for him inside. His body was as thin as a withered branch, but even though he was no longer in active service, his eyes still gleamed with a steely, raptor-like light.

The man had no name. He was known simply as C.

He was the head of the Din Republic's spies, and all directives given to the nation's espionage teams came from him.

Klaus gave his report verbally.

"Well done," C commended him after he finished. "Now those dogs over in the army owe us one. That should make our lives a good deal easier."

"I didn't do this to score points for some internal rivalry."

"Oh, don't be like that. At the end of the day, keeping the army from getting too big for its britches is just another part of maintaining peace for the people."

The Director—which was what Klaus called C—gave Klaus a smile that only went as far as the corners of his mouth.

"Here, let me brew you a cup of coffee."

"No thank you."

"No, I insist. I simply love treating my agents when they finish missions."

Ignoring Klaus's reply, the Director poured some mineral water into his electric kettle and began boiling it.

Klaus gave him an annoyed glower, but the Director continued paying him no heed, instead getting to work grinding the beans.

Klaus sighed and sat down on the sofa.

The Director said nothing during the entire time the coffee took to brew. Then, after delicately preparing two cups, he sat down across from Klaus.

"So just to make absolutely sure," the Director said languidly, "you're certain you want to disband Lamplight?"

"With where the girls are now, they'll be able to return to their academies without problem. They'll be better served by taking thoughtful lessons from skilled instructors, not an incompetent teacher like me."

As Klaus answered, he took a sip of coffee. It tasted about the same as swamp water, but he didn't let his impression show on his face.

"Well, that's a shame." The Director rubbed the back of his neck. "I'd have preferred to keep it around, myself. Can I persuade you to change your mind?"

"Not a chance."

"Based on your last mission, Galgad has its hands on all our nation's information. But a group like Lamplight is made up of problem children they never took notice of; it could serve as our trump card against the Empire."

You're only saying that because you don't know them. Klaus sighed internally.

He admired their skills, but there was still a lot about them that made him worry—in particular, their penchant for making rookie mistakes when they weren't in high gear.

"We can't ask a group of inexperienced girls to put their lives in danger any more than they already have."

"But when you consider the situation our nation faces..."

"The leadership shouldn't be cleaning up their mistakes by forcing grunts to assume greater risk. It isn't a sustainable solution."

That was no way to take responsibility. If the top brass had just caught on to Guido's betrayal, the girls wouldn't have had to clean up after their mess. Looking at the situation objectively, it was downright pathetic.

The only time they were supposed to take on such perilous missions was after they'd developed their strength and skills at their academies. That was just how it worked.

The Director's eye narrowed at Klaus's blunt opinion.

Klaus felt a tingle run across his skin.

Was it annoyance he was sensing? No, it was outright malice.

"...If you want to overrule me, then go ahead. Just don't be surprised when I give you pushback."

"I didn't even say anything yet."

"We're both spies. I can tell how you think."

"...And what if I threatened to gather talented operatives from across the country to force your hand?"

The Director leaned forward and gave Klaus a piercing stare.

It took a commanding presence to control the nation's spies for as long as he had.

"You're welcome to try."

However, Klaus didn't back down. He had no intention of changing his mind, even if his choice meant making enemies out of all his colleagues in the nation.

He returned the Director's gaze with his head held high.

The Director was the first to blink. "...We've already lost Inferno. We can't afford to lose your loyalty, too."

He smiled, then drank his god-awful coffee seemingly with pleasure.

"I guess that's that, then. It is the best way to protect those girls, I suppose."

"I'm extremely grateful to them." Klaus took another sip of his coffee in turn.

"Don't worry, though. Even with Lamplight disbanded, there's nothing to be concerned about. I can keep handling the missions against the Empire just fine by myself."

When the Director heard that, his shoulders slumped uneasily.

"Keeping the Empire at bay wasn't the only reason I wanted to keep Lamplight together, you know."

"How do you mean?"

The Director turned his gaze to his coffee cup, staring at it as though yearning for a long-distant past.

"Inferno's boss used to talk about you a lot. Said you were too dependent on the team."

"What man doesn't love his family?"

"She was worried about you. Said that if you ever lost Inferno, she didn't know if you'd be able to stand on your own two feet."

Klaus pictured his old boss.

After Guido took him in, the one who'd accepted him most warmly was a gentle woman they called Hearth. Many of the things she'd taught him weren't about spy skills but morality.

"…When you put it like that, you make her sound like a mother fretting over how to raise her child."

"Isn't that what she was?"

"………" Klaus said nothing. That was perhaps an affirmation of sorts.

He didn't know how she thought of him, but he certainly saw her as something like a mother. There were times when she was kind and times when she was strict, but she always set his heart at ease. He could still clearly remember all the quieter moments they had shared.

But now she was gone.

And it wasn't just her. He had loved all his teammates, seen them as his brothers and sisters, and now they were—

"You need to take a break, kid." The Director's soft voice echoed in his ears.

"…I have to keep moving forward."

"No. This is one order I'm going to need you to follow."

The Director drank down the rest of his coffee, then stood and placed his hand on Klaus's shoulder.

It felt firm and heavy.

"I'm giving you the next month off. You look like a dead man walking."

"Of course I do. I just lost my family."

"No," the Director disagreed. "It's gotten worse since then."

"........."

Klaus had no rebuttal to that, so he exited the room instead.

By the time he left the Cabinet Office Building, the day had already turned to night.

The sun had long since set, and the moon sat concealed behind a thick drape of clouds. Due to the soot from the city's cotton mills, the night had been especially dark recently. Women and children were rarely found out and about after sundown, but even adult men avoided walking the port city's streets at this time of day. Klaus couldn't help but mentally compare it to the Empire's lavish townscape. It reminded him of just how outmatched the Din Republic was, and he let out a sigh.

He was alone.

He idly gazed up at the overcast sky as he strode down the street.

"........."

His mind was consumed with thoughts of the way he and Guido had parted.

Even after retrieving the bioweapon and securing the girls' escape, Klaus still had one final duty left.

He needed to find out.

Why had Guido betrayed Inferno and led its members to their deaths?

As far as Klaus knew, Guido didn't bear any grudges against the team. Just like Klaus, he loved them and thought of them as his family. So why?

As Guido lay facedown with blood gushing from his back, Klaus went and knelt beside him. Before he could say anything, Guido let out a hoarse murmur.

"You did good, kid…"

"Master…"

There was no sense in getting torn up over how frail Guido's voice was. After all, he had delivered the wounds himself.

"Gotta say, this was a surprise…" Guido smiled weakly. "Never thought I'd get done in by my pupil's pupils…"

"It was all thanks to my brilliant teaching."

"Like hell it was."

Klaus thought of arguing but quickly realized it would be pointless. All the conversations they'd had in Heat Haze Palace had been bugged. Guido knew exactly how terrible Klaus's lessons had been.

"I know how bad you are with words and stuff. You really worked your ass off, didn'tcha?"

"If anyone worked hard, it was the girls. Of course, now that they've beaten you, we'll be parting ways."

"Disbanding, huh? Bet you're gonna be lonely."

"Not at all," Klaus replied. "Not if you come back with me."

"What?" Guido's mouth hung open in disbelief.

Klaus softly touched Guido's throat to check his pulse. "I know it's bad, but I can still give you emergency treatment and save your life."

"Are you for real?"

"Of course, Master. Together, the two of us can rebuild Inferno."

Klaus took off his suit jacket and retrieved the needle and thread stored within its lining. Then, he began slicing it up with a knife to make bandages.

"You're too soft..." Guido watched him in stark disbelief. "Klaus, you idiot... How do you think that's gonna go over with the brass...?"

"The only mission I was tasked with was retrieving the bioweapon, and that's what I did. I won't let them give me a hard time."

"That doesn't mean you can just—"

"You're the only family I have left."

Klaus didn't care if people accused him of letting his emotions dictate his actions. There was a future he wanted, and he didn't care who denounced him on the way there.

However, there was a bare minimum requirement he needed to meet first.

"So please, you have to tell me. Why did you betray the team? Your motive decides your fate."

Klaus gave Guido a pointed look as he heated his needle over a lighter.

Depending on his teacher's answer, that needle would either be used to stitch up his wounds or go straight into his throat.

"Serpent."

The words spilled from Guido's mouth.

"They're a new Imperial spy team, and they're a bunch of creepy fuckers. Made me wanna puke just lookin' at 'em."

"...I've never heard of them."

"They came to me and—"

"Master, be quiet for a minute." Klaus cut him off.

Now that he knew there were circumstances outside of Guido's control, his top priority was getting him stable.

"I'm going to do some basic surgery now. I can tell you had your reasons. Once we get back—"

However, Klaus never got a chance to say *You can tell me all the details.*

As he leaned forward, a bullet came flying.

He had sensed no enemies. No noise.

Even for Klaus, stitching up a wound in lighting conditions that poor required a fair bit of concentration. His entire focus had been directed at his dying mentor. He had no chance to react to the bullet aimed right between his eyes.

He was wide open. It was the perfect surprise attack.

I'm going to die.

The moment after reaching that conclusion, blood splattered all around him.

His entire body was covered in red.

"Master...?"

And Guido was lying on top of him.

The moment he realized Guido had taken the bullet for him, he also realized that the liquid he was covered in was Guido's blood. The bullet had hit him square in the chest.

When Guido's body slumped off him, Klaus got a clear look.

In the distance, on a rooftop, a person was holding a rifle.

The sniper turned around and disappeared into the shadows.

Klaus had no intention of giving chase. He pressed down on Guido's wound to stanch the bleeding. Guido's life was fading away before his eyes, and he had to stop it.

However, he knew he was already too late.

Guido let out a whisper. "———"

After those final words, he never spoke again.

When Klaus got back to Heat Haze Palace, he didn't see a single soul there.

The only noise echoing through the manor was the sound of him opening and closing the door.

His mind raced with thoughts about the mysterious spy team Serpent, and he had no desire to devote the next month to relaxation. He wanted revenge, and as a spy, he felt a sense of obligation, too. He needed to investigate.

When he tried to ascend the stairs to his bedroom, though, his feet came to a stop. The Director was right—he was exhausted. He would need to get at least *some* rest.

He headed to the main hall and sat down on a sofa.

From his seat beneath the grandfather clock, he had a clear view of the entire room.

It had been a while since he last sat there.

Back when Inferno lived in Heat Haze Palace, that was his usual spot. He often liked to nod off in it, and whenever he came back from a life-or-death mission, he would always sit on that sofa to set his heart at ease. When he looked up, he would find the boss had brewed him some tea, one of the other members was baking financiers, and Guido had gone to buy cheesecake. Then, he and his teammates would shoot the breeze and thank one another for their hard work.

Ever since Inferno had disappeared and Lamplight had replaced it, though, the main hall had become a room that he simply passed through. Maybe he should have spent more time with the girls. Some nights, when he came down through the main hall to get some tea, he would hear their heated discussions. Their goal was to polish their skills however they could in order to beat him. At times, that took the form of arguing; others, it manifested as mutual encouragement. Klaus had some concerns about the fact that they'd failed to notice their target—him—passing through the main hall, grabbing tea leaves from the cabinet in the kitchen nearby and leaving, but he remembered clearly how much he had looked forward to seeing how they would attack him the following day.

There were no end to the memories this place held for him.

He treasured the time he'd shared with Inferno, and the days he'd spent with Lamplight hadn't been half bad, either.

But now he was alone.

Both of those eras were lost to him.

"It feels so empty…"

It felt odd, sitting alone in a room that used to be so full of laughter.

What was that emotion eating away at his heart?

His plan had gone perfectly. His work was worthy of the moniker Guido had given him—the World's Greatest.

He'd completed his mission, hadn't let a single teammate die, and had dealt with the traitor who'd destroyed Inferno.

He had even devised a method to get around his inability to teach.

Surely, no one else could have achieved all that.

So why wasn't he satisfied?

"Was this…?" Klaus said aloud. "Was this really the ending I wanted?"

In the final analysis, what had the last two months really been good for?

Then, just as the lament left his lips, he noticed something.

He couldn't move his right arm.

Was it bound?

By wire? Since when?

By the time he realized something was off, it was already too late to react.

A vast web of wires snaked out from behind the sofa, ensnaring his neck, legs, torso, and head, one after another, and preventing him from moving.

At first, he considered trying to evade them. That was when he noticed the gun muzzles pointed his way.

As a matter of fact, he was surrounded. The girls had emerged from behind the furniture.

The black- and white-haired ladies were pointing their guns at his flanks, their brown-haired partner was aiming at his legs, and the red-haired member was leveling her gun straight at his heart. The pink-haired girl was watching over the proceedings with delight, and her cerulean-haired comrade was watching them coolly. Klaus couldn't see the blond—Erna—so he assumed she was standing behind the sofa.

"We finally got you!"

Their silver-haired ringleader—Lily—wasn't doing much of anything, but she stood before him and threw out her chest proudly all the same.

"You...you're all supposed to be back at your academies by now..."

"Oh, that was just an act," Lily replied nonchalantly.

What had prompted the change of heart?

For several days now, the girls had been making preparations to return to their spy academies with referrals from Klaus. They had even thrown a going-away party the very night prior.

"Heh-heh, victory is finally ours. Now we can make you follow whatever demand we want!"

"And what demand is that?"

"Isn't it obvious? We want to stay together as Lamplight," Lily announced confidently.

Klaus wanted to tilt his head to the side, but the wires wrapped around him made that impossible.

"But why? When we first met, you made the exact opposite—"

"Yup, and I'm the exact opposite Lily as I was back then."

Lily made a peace sign in front of her face, then wiggled her two upright fingers back and forth as she proudly elaborated.

"We talked it out among ourselves, see. And it's, like, instead of going back to school and graduating and getting put on some spy team full of strangers, we'd all rather stick with the teammates we've already gone through trials and tribulations with."

"That's not unreasonable, but..." Klaus couldn't help but nod; Lily was coming on terribly strong.

That much all made sense, but there were still some things he didn't understand.

"...Why bother tricking me, tying me up, and holding me at gunpoint when you could have asked normally?"

"We're just picking up your lesson where we left off."

"The lesson ended a while ago, though."

"Oh. Call it payback, then."

"You really do have a warped personality."

That could be a useful trait for a spy, but it made Lily more than a bit of a handful.

She beamed at him, tickled pink by her victory.

"Hee-hee. Complain all you like, it's not gonna help. We've got a hostage, too."

"What?"

"Take a look."

Their white-haired member gave the wire some slack for a moment to show Klaus what was beneath the sofa.

At some point, they had moved his canvas there. Because of where it was placed, any violent moves would destroy it under their feet.

"It's the painting you spent so long working on. If you're not careful, it'll get totally ruined."

"You're a monster."

"See how much stronger we've gotten? And we have one person to thank for that." Lily gently extended her hand. "That's why we want you to keep teaching us. Teach us how a bunch of washouts like us can come into bloom."

The other girls all followed up by chiming in as well.

"Training with you was the best training I've ever done," they said, and "Yo, samesies!" and "You're the one who helped me get closer to my dream, Teach," and "I've admired Inferno for so long, I can imagine no better teacher"...

One after another, they all told him how much they trusted him.

Guido's last words lingered in Klaus's mind.

"Make sure you protect 'em this time."

It was his final order before breathing his last.

Klaus had followed that instruction and tried to get the girls as far away from his missions as possible. Sending them back to their spy academies was his way of protecting them. Now, though, he realized he had been going about it all wrong. The myriad techniques being wound around his body showed him that. The girls had grown.

He might not be able to teach, but he was still their teacher.

The choice he had to make was clear.

"All righty, Teach! You ready to say *I surrender*?" Lily's voice still rang with pride. "Agree to let Lamplight keep operating, say you surrender, and while you're at it, maybe apologize for trouncing us so badly each—"

"One question—," Klaus asked. "How much longer should I keep playing along with this game?"

He ripped his way through the girls' restraints.

Taking advantage of the moment they were most assured of victory, he pulled hard on the wires. The girls holding them in place lost their balance, and the swinging wires mowed the rest of the girls down as well. Their guns probably didn't have live ammo anyway, but they never got a chance to shoot. Fear of friendly fire made them hesitate, and that gave Klaus time to use the restraints to snatch their guns away.

It wasn't the cleanest solution, but he was working with what he had.

Not having seen his counterattack coming, Lamplight was caught completely off guard. Klaus stepped all over his canvas as he ensured his students were immobile. They still lacked experience. Clearly, more training was in order.

Beneath his feet, the canvas was a shredded mess.

"T-Teach, why would you go so far?! You destroyed your precious painting!"

"Just now, I decided to stop fixating on the past," he replied with conviction.

His desire for revenge wasn't about to just up and vanish, of course. But he had discovered a new path he could take.

If all that awaited him after exacting his vengeance was a big house with nobody in it, then that was too lonely a future to bear.

Surely the boss wouldn't have minded. His master and the rest of his team would have approved, too.

"You all aren't qualified to be my enemies," Klaus casually remarked.

They weren't his enemies.

He doubted they ever could be.

But perhaps they could become something else...

Life was full of irony.

He had spent the last few months working to avenge his team but in doing so had obtained an entirely new one.

Klaus gathered up his mangled painting and tore a strip of dried paint off it. Then, after locating a blank spot on the main hall's wall, he pressed the dry paint against it and drew a single line. It was thin, red, and fleeting, yet it was powerful all the same.

Now he was finished.

Klaus compared the two paintings.

One of them, the violent mess of red paint titled "Family," was like a blazing inferno.

The other, painted from a single piece ripped from the first to create something new, was like a faint lamplight.

"Magnificent."

Klaus smiled.

He could come up with a name for the new piece later.

Now the room he had once shared with his family was adorned with a painting of his new team.

Afterword

It's nice to meet you. I'm Takemachi, Grand Prize winner of the 32nd Fantasia Taisho awards.

I submitted this under the title *The Spy's Sweet Temptations—All the Other Students Are Beautiful Girls*. From there, the book went through a number of revisions, and now it's in the form you see today.

Incidentally, the reason the actual book's synopsis turned out so different from my submission's is because of conversations I had with my editor. After analyzing the story's strengths and weaknesses, I rewrote it to better live up to the expectations that winning the Grand Prize carries. And if anyone bought this book hoping to use it as a reference for their own future Fantasia Taisho submissions, don't worry. Anything you may have heard about the editorial department poisoning me or blackmailing me into making changes is a lie. All they did was offer me delicious coffee and win me over through gentle persuasion.

If anyone's curious about the original synopsis, please feel free to check it out on the Fantasia Taisho website. If you do, you'll be able to see just how much work went into the revisions—mostly on my editor's part.

Starting here, I have some people to thank.

To Tomari, the book's illustrator, thank you for giving the characters such great designs. Klaus, in particular, was so cool, he gave me shivers. Some of the girls didn't get much of a spotlight this time around, but I'll make sure to change that in the next book so your fantastic designs for them get a chance to shine.

To Asaura, who helped me research the book's firearms, I can't thank you enough for helping get a gun novice like me up to speed. Now that you've taught me how much there is to know, I feel like I'm ready to start learning more.

To the Fantasia Taisho selection committee, thank you so much for awarding me your prestigious Grand Prize. As I mentioned before, the actual book ended up being pretty different from my submission, and it's all thanks to the responsibility with which you entrusted me that I was able to make so many changes.

And finally, to all my readers. I know that "spies" isn't the most common theme for a light novel, so thank you for reading my book anyway. The next volume should be coming out soon, so I hope to see you again then.

Until next time.

Takemachi